Junk Food Hero

Pat Swindells

AURORA METRO PRESS

Thanks to: Aidan Jenkins, Judy Heckstall-Smith, Simon
Bennett, Neil Gregory, Carmel Walsh, Gabriele Maurer,
Cordelia Makartsev

Production: Gillian Wakeling

ISBN 978 1-906582-02-9 Printed by Ashford Colour
Press, Fareham, UK.

To the memory of Tony
without whose expertise and encouragement
none of my books would have
ever reached completion
and with loving thanks to
Duncan, Georgia and Corin for
always being there for me.

FIRST COURSE

The Rebel

It is sometimes said that heroes appear in all shapes and sizes. If they do, remarkably few of them appear in the shape (roughly spherical) or size (extra extra large) of thirteen-year-old George Guzell who weighed seventeen and a half stone while still growing in all directions.

Heroes do *not* usually have big bellies and fat necks or open-pored complexions. They are not generally as thick as the proverbial two short planks. Although they are sometimes obsessed, it is rarely with *food*. Nevertheless, George was destined to become a hero. Exactly how he accomplished this makes a strange but helpful story which I shall now relate.

It must be admitted that George never gave the smallest indication to anyone that, one day, he would achieve the lofty status of hero. In fact, most people who knew him would have said he was the *least* likely teenager to do any such thing. Some people thought he was boring, others thought him repulsive. A few despised him for his complete lack of willpower.

Of course, there were those who took the uncharitable view that he was not so much congenitally fat, as congenitally greedy. And while George tried to ignore his vast unpopularity, the unpalatable fact was that George did not particularly like himself.

It was George's firmly held belief that his body needed a constant intake of food, which is why, on the day our story begins, unable to wait one moment longer for the school dinner bell to ring, he had puffed and panted his way from school to chippy. Upon his return, he stuffed the last handful of chips into his mouth, dropped the empty paper into a bin and turned his attention to the inviting, savoury smells ahead. Perfect timing!

Lurching lopsidedly towards the end of the dinner queue, George left a trail of scattered chairs and tables in his wake. Unmoved by the shouts of protest that followed him, there was just one thing on his mind – the day's menu.

Meals at Worthington Knight Comprehensive School had been a big disappointment since the recent visit of Manx-born TV chef and restaurateur Del Dingley or "Salad Man" as George contemptuously called him. To George, a "balanced diet" meant a hamburger in each hand, and no salad. As he reached the end of the queue, he neared the platform where the staff were busy eating and where the imposing figure of "Gruff", the Headmaster, stared unblinkingly down the length of the dining hall.

"I've got my eye on you," Gruff had once said to George and George felt that he still had. Even today, as his position in the queue gradually improved, he imagined himself to be the target of Gruff's attention the centre of his bull's-eye.

However, he was quite wrong. Robert Canterbury Knight, the Head, had not even noticed him. Although he enjoyed giving the impression that he was all-seeing and all-hearing, the truth was quite different. For a moment, his eyes dwelt fondly on the dining hall's warm, walnut panelling, original features of a one-time Victorian Ragged School. Founded as a charitable institution for poor children, the school continued to benefit from the will of one Worthington Knight, distant ancestor of the Head.

Although payment of one such seasonal legacy was about due, Mr Knight's mind had been distracted from consideration of how to distribute the funds, to the more urgent question of the staff and pupils' reaction to the new menu. Del Dingley's new thinking (or was it old thinking with its sleeves rolled up?) had not been an unqualified success. Good ideas needed a sound landing strip as well as wings if they were to take flight.

Signed petitions and deputations to both the staff and the School Council had followed actively hostile demonstrations. The fact that some pupils went along with the new food was no consolation. Lunch had become a ticking time-bomb, the tension was palpable. "Any sign of uprising amongst the natives, Headmaster?" He was joined by his Deputy, Jack Champion.

"Thankfully, no! Though I had one or two pertinent letters in this morning's mailbag. Usual stuff! Children must have what they want to eat, whenever and wherever they like, no questions asked etc... Don't they read the information we send home? Or don't they care?"

Jack Champion uttered a humourless laugh. "When it comes to personal freedom, people care a great deal. Eating, drinking and smoking, despite the risks, are all part of that freedom. Freedom to be bloody-minded, if you like."

From his place in the dinner queue, George observed the two men in conversation. Although he feared Gruff, it was the presence of Mr Champion which really terrified him. Involuntarily, he straightened up a bit, trying in vain to tighten the sagging muscles of his belly, whilst concentrating on not catching Champion's eye. The two men watched the restless line of boys and girls waiting for food. For the present, all seemed quiet. No disruption in the queue lining up at the serving hatch. No loud displays of dissatisfaction at the tables. Perhaps the trouble-makers had already decamped to the local chippy or to the burger van parked round the corner. Satisfied that all was well, Mr Knight returned to his table and accepted the Tuna Crisp placed before him. It looked good... Tasted excellent... Full marks to Mrs. Dulgence, the cook, who had given it her best shot.

Mr Knight watched as George approached the serving hatch and engaged the cook in conversation. Her folded arms suggested she was none too pleased with the way things were developing.

"Trouble, Headmaster?" Jack Champion materialised immediately. "Not Guzell again?" The Deputy's mouth tightened at the sound of raised voices; it was most unusual for the cook to lose her temper.

"No! I won't!" George's voice rang out loud and clear. He pointed a threatening finger at the neatly written lunch menu.

"Chicken Curry – dog poo!" Loud giggles from the rest of the queue. "Tuna Crisp. Yuck!" More laughter. "Fish Pie!" George made retching sounds so realistic that several teachers put down their knives and forks and stared.

Jack Champion leapt off the platform, covering the distance in six strapping strides. Yet he was not the first. The dinner queue had already disgorged the petite figure of Miss Jemima Walker, Head of Geography, and currently on dinner duty. "Enough of that, George! That's insulting to Mrs. Dulgence." The cook was looking flushed and almost on the verge of tears. "Apologise, at once."

"No!" George's answer was unequivocal. "Why should I?" And in all honesty – and ignorance – he didn't know why he should. He stared belligerently at the woman behind the counter and then, as an after-thought, at Miss Walker. "It's my food," he told them. "My dinner. I paid for it and I ought to get what I want to eat. It's not like other things in school where I've got to do what you lot say. It's not the same." He didn't know how to explain exactly what he meant but clearly the rest of the queue had no difficulty understanding and supported him with shrill whistles and stamping feet.

The Deputy Head had halted close by to assess the situation. He was surprised to find himself slightly in agreement with some of the boy's thinking, badly expressed though it was. Food wasn't really a school issue, was it? Well, it never had been up to now. He cringed as he heard the newly qualified Miss Walker taking a different tack. "Be fair, George. You voted that we should all give this a try."

The boy went from pink to puce in seconds. Definitely not Miss Walker's finest hour. "I didn't! I didn't! I didn't!" The words spat out with a spray of spit.

"Actually, George, you did," Mr Champion intervened. He turned to his younger colleague and whispered. A nod of thanks and Miss Walker returned to her duties, at the other end of the hall.

"I didn't!" The boy blinked. Tears threatened. The fire had gone out of him, leaving his skin ashen and sweating.

"We all did," the Deputy Head corrected. He spoke quietly, but there was no suggestion of compromise. "We all had a vote." George gulped to steady himself.

"Not me! I voted against it." He was surprised to hear muttered murmurings of agreement. Were they agreeing with him? Some of the girls were actually nodding their heads and clapping. Nelson Ward even went so far as to slap George's back with one hand while delivering a surreptitious two-fingered salute in the direction of the kitchen. George wasn't used to gaining support from anybody, least of all the members of his class.

"If you remember, we all agreed to abide by the majority vote. You…" Mr Champion paused. "You and a lot of other people who thought as you did – lost – including Ward here who will be enjoying the pleasure of my company a little later in the day. So George, you must agree to give the food a chance. Up to now, there's not been much evidence of that."

He looked across the counter where Mrs. Dulgence had regained her normal, unruffled appearance but was clearly upset by the stream of pupils who were taking one look at her healthy menu and heading straight for the doors. "What's the problem here then, Dot?" Mr Champion asked, lightly.

Dot's smile embraced them both. "It's no chips for George, today," she informed him, pleasantly.

"Just so! We all agreed chips once a week. Your day?" He looked at George who chose not to reply. "Tuesday," Mrs. Dulgence had consulted a list behind the counter.

"And today is Wednesday. So, as they say, you've had your chips for this week." He looked for an answering smile. But George had no intention of being mollified. Champion tried again. "Apologise to Mrs. Dulgence, George. Choose something from the menu without any chips today, and," he paused significantly, "we'll say no more about it." He turned back to the counter. "Now, what have we on offer, Mrs. Dulgence?"

"Fish Pie…"

George's howl of agony drowned the rest of her suggestions and could be heard the length and breadth of the dining hall. It was like an animal in pain. "I'm not eating fish pie or any other muck! I WANT MY CHIPS!"

"Right! That's it." George felt one of Champion's hands on the collar of his blazer and the other tightening on the folds at the back of his jacket. To have seized the seat of his pants would have been quite impossible as the seat of George's pants was skin-tight and fold-free. "Out!" said Champion.

"Get off!" George shouted and fought.

Now the Head was certainly watching him. From the staff table, Mr Knight saw his Deputy man-handle the snivelling, protesting boy out of the dining hall and into the quietness of the corridor where he would, presumably, try to reach some sort of compromise.

What remained of the queue moved forward again to the accompaniment of overly-loud sighs of relief and comments about empty bellies.

On their way to collect – or reject a Dingley/Dulgence dinner, every student paused for a moment to stir a giant pudding mixture in a huge cauldron. It was "Stir Up Wednesday": the school's own version of the traditional "Stir Up Sunday". Today, the whole school was taking turns to stir the swirling mass of organic pudding without which no Christmas celebration could ever be complete.

Contrary to popular belief, the mixture now being enthusiastically churned by members of the Lower School was not the same as the one they would consume at that year's Christmas dinner. Mrs. Dulgence and her army of dinner ladies cooked the new pudding but served "the one they'd made earlier". Thus, the school was guaranteed a rich, moist, full-fruited offering which had been maturing for twelve months.

As far as the pupils were concerned, size was everything. Let Mrs. Dulgence worry about quality; what really counted was that the pudding be large enough to be paraded, with due pomp and circumstance, before the multitude – a mouth-watering pageant.

This year, it was especially important to make the Christmas meal doubly enjoyable. Mr Knight used the remaining lunch break to check his table plan, the positioning of the Christmas tree and other decorations.

SECOND COURSE

George In The Looking Glass

Meanwhile, outside the dining-hall, Jack Champion had swiftly removed the still protesting George to the privacy of his study. He waited, shuffled some papers around his desk and only when loud gulps announced the cessation of the protestation did he bother to speak. "Sit down, George!"

"I don't want to sit down." The man raised an eyebrow and George reluctantly added, "sir". But there was no mistaking the belligerence in George's declaration, "I want my chips! And you can't stop me."

"Well, you can't have them. Whether or not I can stop you is, perhaps, a moot point." He hoped that George didn't understand the word "moot." "If we let you do whatever you like," Champion walked around the office, emphasizing who was boss, "every other boy or girl who voted as you did – and lost – will expect the same – chips on demand. Now! Do as I tell you. Sit down!" George sat, with the maximum noise and scraping of chair legs. Jack Champion remained unimpressed. "Let's see if we can talk this through like two reasonable human beings."

"I was most disappointed by your behaviour in the dining-hall, today, George." (As if I care, thought George.) "Your reactions were extremely childish... I shall be watching you closely in the future, George." (Big deal, thought George, who was still too angry to realise this might be a good time to back down.) "And," continued Mr Champion, "I shall be hoping for a big improvement. Throwing a tantrum is never the answer. Nature gave you two ends – one to sit on and one to think with. Your success or failure in life will depend upon which one you use the most... Do you have anything to say?"

George could have said plenty, but as it included several four-letter words and featured a plate of fat-laden chips, he chose the silent option. Fixing his eyes on the floor and taking good care neither to speak nor to meet the master's questioning gaze, he waited. (Perhaps "sir" might let him off with a warning.)

But Mr Champion had other ideas, now. He removed a mirror from the wall and shoved it, none too gently, onto the boy's lap. "Who's that?" George looked away. Jack Champion raised the mirror closer until George had no choice but to consider his reflection. "I say again, George: who is that?"

"Me, of course." He didn't want to look. He knew only too well what the mirror would show: perspiring, spot-ridden skin bulging from ear to ear like a mask without folds.

"Yes, you, of course. And are you satisfied with what you see?"

"It doesn't matter whether I am or I'm not." He took care not to meet the teacher's eyes, afraid of the intensity of his own emotion. "I'm me. I'm what I am." He shrugged his shoulders, cockily pretending an aggression he no longer felt.

"You're quite right." Mr Champion agreed. "You are what you are. It's not how you started, though. It's what you have become. And what really concerns me is what you may become, if you don't do something about it. Heart disease, strokes, diabetes, any or all of these things." George tried to shut out all this extra, unasked-for information. (Why do teachers have to go on and on and on?) But there was no stopping Champion in full flow. "According to those who know about these things, you're what is called "fat". And you're not the only one. This school, indeed this town, is full of people who have allowed themselves to become seriously overweight."

"Can't help that! Can't help being fat! It's an illness. Not my fault." George mumbled away into the top of his collar. "It's my glands. My mum says I've got fatty tubes." George waited for this start-ling fact to amaze his teacher.

Years of straight-face practice helped Jack Champion not to laugh. "Well! Far be it from me to contradict your mum, George, but in all honesty, any doctor or health club would be unhappy with that diagnosis. You're fat. That is what they would say. Fat, lad. Face it. And remember this – and think about it: if you could kick the bottom of the person who is most responsible for your fatness, you wouldn't be able to sit down for a week."

"I'll bring my mum up to you, sir. You'll see!

She'll tell you!" George was hopping mad.

"Please do." Mr Champion could not have been more correct or more untruthful, "I always enjoy meeting parents."

He ignored George's aside: "You'd not enjoy meeting mine."

"As I said, I always enjoy meeting parents, especially so when we have a mutual problem. After all, she must be just as worried about you as we at the school are."

"I'm just saying what she says – she and my dad." He felt suddenly nervous about the whole idea of his parents meeting Mr Champion.

"And are those fatty tubes," Mr Champion enquired, "inherited?"

Although there had been nothing to suggest that the teacher was amused – no quirky smile – no hint of laughter, George still had the feeling that he was being mocked.

"It's not a joke." His voice was serious and he contrived to look hurt.

"No, indeed," agreed Jack Champion. "Far from it. I think that is the point I have been trying to make, without too much success, ever since you came in."

"Imagine if you had fatty tubes, sir." George continued, "You'd want people to like you for what you are." Vaguely, he remembered hearing somebody somewhere saying something like that.

"I couldn't agree more. In the final analysis, it's who we are that really counts." George perked up. That was what he had been trying to say. "But, George, if you want to be liked by others, you have to work at it. And you start by asking yourself the question: am I likeable as I am? If the answer is "no", you have to do something about it ... the first step is always the same: you must say to yourself, "I'll try – ". Every achievement, great or small starts with "I'll try – " and then you do it." There was a short pause while Mr Champion eyed George's flabby, powerless physique. "You may as well face up to your problems, George... You can't run fast enough or far enough to get away from them."

Mr Champion had a dim recollection of the last parents' night when a couple had waddled in, huffing and puffing, to commandeer the first available chairs, where they remained anchored all night. George's parents – Ivor and Nora Guzell – fat and formidable! Hereditary glandular problems… Unlikely! George's obesity and that of his parents had probably been acquired from their unhealthy life-style, rather than inherited from their ancestors.

For the moment, though, he had to be satisfied that he and George had reached an uneasy sort of truce. Aloud, he said, "Well, George, we can't have you going into lessons without some food. That's a recipe for disaster if I ever heard one. It's one the Headmaster won't accept." George wriggled uncomfortably at the mention of Mr Knight. The last thing he wanted was an eyeball-to-eyeball with old Gruff. "Do you want to take this as far as the Headmaster, George?" Champion had noticed and seized upon his discomfort. "Or do you think we can sort it, if only for today?"

"Mr Knight is very busy, sir. Perhaps it would be better not to bother him." Champion paused as though considering the point, then nodded slowly. But he couldn't persuade George to try any of the healthy options on the menu.

Back in the dining room, he watched George's half-hearted apology to Mrs Dulgence and reluctant acceptance of her newly made beef burgers. Less fat. Less salt. Some of the salt-and-fat fancying pupils would probably have said "and less taste, too." On the question of chips, Mr Champion would not budge and George had to settle for a chunk of wholesome granary bread.

The afternoon was a misery for George – all he wanted out of afternoon school was himself. Yet his attempts to doze were repeatedly frustrated by his noisy classmates. "Guzell's being gross, Miss!" shouted Sally Larkin, as George's stomach rumbled and belched right through Miss Walker's lesson on the plight of Third World countries. George was much more concerned with his own shortages. Beef burgers and bread had done nothing to fill the aching void that was used to three – nay, four times that quantity. The only consolation was the thought of Mr Champion going head to head with his mum. He almost felt sorry for the man. (But only "almost".) Weighing in at eighteen and a half stones, with fists like a super heavy-weight and a mouth to match, she was an equal for anyone, including Champion. His mum had always been a powerful speaker and often a simple argument had ended with her adversary thumped, bruised or bleeding.

❀❀❀❀❀

"What shall we do?" Jack Champion stood alongside the Headmaster as they watched, from the Head's first-floor room, the school's departure at four o'clock. "He's not a bad lad, really." He spoke slowly, as if trying to convince himself.

The two men watched George's progress as he lurched along to the school gates. The only thing that George did quickly was get tired. He was so slow that his self-winding watch kept stopping. At the gates, he immediately sat on a wall to wait for the bus. Knight frowned in his direction. "Look at him, for God's sake. He can barely move. That's what he should be doing." He pointed to a boisterous group of boys engaged in the energetic leapings and shoutings which normally accompany release from school. "And look at them!" His voice rose as he spotted some girls gyrating about and expending huge amounts of energy as they combined talking, turning and twirling to attract the attention of passing upper school boys.

Champion laughed. "He couldn't if he tried." He paused. "You know I actually felt quite sorry for him today. Didn't want to look at himself in the mirror. And trotted out all that garbage about his fat being hereditary."

The Head turned, sharply. "Is it? Garbage?" Champion nodded. "I don't want to get this wrong," Knight persisted. There was no mistaking the concern or the challenge. "Let's not forget Karen." Both men fell silent as they remembered one of the school's most successful and popular students. Karen Paxton had been a pretty girl with a vibrant personality but coping with a genetic disorder which made it impossible for her to control her massively overweight body. "So, I ask you again, Jack. Are you sure?"

"The whole family is grossly overweight, and there's never been anything in the school doctor's report to suggest that the cause is anything other than self-indulgence of the first order."

Turning away from the window, the Head, looking even more thoughtful than usual, reached for the key to a small cabinet and poured a couple of modest sherries. "If I'm being truthful, Jack, I'm not too sure about some of this, myself." His Deputy was startled. It was rare for the Boss to admit to any misgivings. "Until now, we've had clear lines of demarcation between home and school," Jack Champion pricked up his ears, "food being very much the responsibility of the parents and education, in the academic sense, being down to us. I never used to worry about what went into school dinners. I thought of them as a stop-gap until kids got home for a proper meal. But now, I find that lots of them haven't been fed properly either at school or at home. And if Del Dingley is to be believed, even pupils of normal weight could be lacking in essential body-building nutrients, through eating junk food."

Champion sipped his sherry. "I don't see what we can expect to achieve unless the parents do something about it, too."

There was a long silence. "Perhaps we should talk to George's mother," said the Head, slowly and reluctantly.

"You've seen her," Champion grimaced. The Head looked doubtful. "Course you have. That awful woman who demonstrated outside the school gates. Weighs a ton. Looks like a Sumo wrestler. Nora Guzell. The mother from hell. Young George was threatening me earlier with a visitation."

"Worried?" Robert Knight's eyes crinkled with amusement. This was a new side to his Deputy.

"Frankly, yes." They both laughed. "She could fell me with a look, never mind a blow." Champion consulted his watch. "Sorry, Headmaster. Must dash."

George was no longer at the bus stop. The thought of a five minute journey without sustenance was not to be borne. Showing considerably more energy than he'd demonstrated all day, George puffed his way round the corner and producing a fist full of small coins, treated himself to some salt and vinegar crisps and several bars of chocolate from the local sweet shop.

THIRD COURSE

The TV Programme

George took the bus home. All of three stops. Just time enough to polish off the crisps and make substantial inroads into the chocolate. Stuffing his mouth, he stared sightlessly through the windows, his mind still occupied with the events of the day. Once again, he'd managed to get himself on the wrong side of the teaching staff. Even though he'd gone through the motions of apologising to Mrs Dulgence, he couldn't help feeling that they had no right to tell him what he should and shouldn't eat. It had been nice that some people had spoken up for him and he chuckled as he thought about Nelson's comment. He felt, again, a warm glow as he recalled that rare moment of peer approval. Some of the girls had even applauded.

Once off the crowded bus, he decided to pay his gran a visit. She could be relied on for sweet tea, chocolate cake and sympathy. His salivary glands worked overtime as he thought about her three-inch-deep sponge cake with its filling of chocolate butter cream and rich white icing.

He'd barely closed the garden gate before the cottage door opened. Prudence Guzell had half-expected him today, as – indeed – most days. For the last quarter of an hour she had been looking out for him. Nobody was more aware than the old lady of the loneliness of her grandson but now there was something else – something she couldn't identify. She was used to his slipshod, untidy appearance. What can you expect from a child who weighs seventeen and a half stone and is still growing? But she wasn't used to the drooping shoulders and hanging head. What had gone wrong this time? Her face, though, reflected nothing of her concern and her smile was entirely predictable. George felt that here, at any rate, everything was okay.

"Gran!" His hug told her so much.

"George!" She returned a kiss. "Lovely to see you. Come on in." An arm still about him, she led him into the cheery, little sitting room where an open log fire leapt flames up the chimney, casting a rosy glow around the room.

George dumped his satchel and collapsed into his accustomed seat by the fire, leaving the large, old rocker on the far side for Gran. They sat in companionable silence for a while. "Everything okay, George?" Gran was leaning forward and looking at him, quite anxiously. "You seem a bit down."

He started to say "I'm fine!" but the words drifted away and with the sentence unfinished he just sat there staring at the fire. He felt strangely embarrassed at the thought of telling Gran about his earlier outburst in the dining hall. To avoid her penetrating gaze, he got up and moved around the room, touching photos and familiar bric-a-brac, expecting that at any moment she would challenge him.

Granny Guzell had known far too many boys in her lifetime not to know when one of them was lying. To give herself time to think and also to see what George would do or say next, she excused herself and went to the kitchen. For the next few minutes, the sound of kettle and cups heralded the arrival of tea and a large slice of the favourite cake. In the sitting room, she could hear George padding around, picking up this and that but replacing them with rather more than his usual care.

When she returned, she found George standing by the piano, looking at the family picture gallery. "Who's that? This little man in uniform?"

Prudence smiled. "That, George, is your Great Grandfather, Mortimer Guzell." A snigger escaped George. What kind of a name was that?

"George!" George recognised the warning that he should not make fun of distant relatives, especially ones who had fought for King and country in World War Two. "I never knew him. His own son never knew him. But Myrtle – your Great Grandmother – used to tell amazing tales about him." George raised a questioning eyebrow. "He survived Dunkirk and was killed on D-Day at the Normandy landings."

They stood in silence, both thinking about what that meant. To Prue, the whole concept of war was so much easier. She had lived through one war and seen the devastation and heartbreak when friends and relations didn't come back.

To George, it was a difficult concept to get his head around. He'd seen fighting on telly and at the cinema but there was always that flat screen creating a barrier between himself and reality.

He tried to imagine how Great Grandfather had got himself killed. Shot? Machine gunned? Blown-up? Crushed by a tank?

"Missing, presumed dead." Gran told him in a matter of fact sort of way. "I've got the telegram somewhere."

George wasn't sure that he wanted to see it. "What was he really like? He looks tough. I suppose he was brave." Pride stirred as he thought about his dead relation.

"Well, I think anybody who lived through the war and fought in it had got to be tough just to survive. Think about it, George. Where you live now there was once a row of little houses. All blown to pieces in 1940."

"And this. Who's this?" George had moved on to the next photo.

Granny Guzell frowned. "You know who it is. Why do you keep asking me who it is? Every time you come you ask the same question. It's your dad just before he came out of the army."

"He looks…" George stood and stared, as he had done every day for the last few weeks, "sort of fit and sunburnt and…" His voice faltered.

"Slim! Of course he does. He'd just spent two years getting fit. The army's no rest cure, you know. All that physical exercise and marching. As for the suntan: three months in Cyprus saw to that." She returned to her chair by the fire.

George followed her and sat down, watching her pouring the tea and slicing the cake. "So what happened?" He just couldn't believe the difference in the Dad of the photo and the Dad he saw every day at home.

"He came home, of course. Oh, you mean what happened to him?" She guessed that, like all the other times recently, he was really asking about his father's changed appearance. "Oh, lots of things. A sedentary occupation." He was not familiar with the word. "A sitting-down job – Print Costing and Estimating – for a big printing company." She didn't like to add "fags, booze, and convenience foods."

Mentally, George added two of them for her. Very slowly, he thought it through. Fags! He pictured overflowing ashtrays and the panic when fags ran out and the local shops were shut. Booze! He'd never seen his parents drunk but he wondered if he had ever seen them completely sober, either.

But there was another factor troubling Granny Guzell – one she could not easily put into words. She definitely couldn't say, "And your mam happened."

"Is Dad o...o... oby... something?" It was a word George kept hearing bandied about at school. It was a word that scared him. Perhaps, if he didn't get to know it, then it couldn't be true of him... Whatever it was.

"Obese." Obligingly, the old lady finished for him, although she wished it hadn't cropped up. Afraid of putting her foot in it, she said, "I'm not too sure what "obese" really means. Your dad's obviously overweight, but obese – I wouldn't have thought so." Surprised by the fear in George's eyes, she changed the subject. For the rest of the visit, she kept the boy interested with tales of the 40s and 50s, a mixture of wartime reminiscences and, as memories of her own dead husband came flooding back, stories of her own youth and marriage in a society bearing no relationship to the one in which George now lived.

At last, George crammed down the final piece of chocolate cake, drained his beaker and, giving Gran a perfunctory kiss, set off for home, leaving behind an extremely worried old lady. She would have liked to ring her son, Ivor, and express her concern but past experience had taught her that this was definitely not an option. While Nora had strong views about mothers-in-law who interfered, Ivor never exerted himself enough to have strong views about anything.

The house was nearly in darkness by the time George reached home. Every curtain was drawn and only the smallest of lamps illuminated the sitting-room, which held what had to be the largest, slim-line and most comprehensively channelled TV currently available. As usual, it was turned on full blast. Every nook and cranny of the house sported a TV or a PC, banishing any inclination for physical activity. Unless you counted shopping, when the mouse could be mobilised with consummate dexterity.

George usually divided his time between TV and PC, doing what bit of homework took his fancy, with a book on his knees while he watched the big screen.

There was no greeting as he entered the room. No enquiries about how the day had gone. Not a wave of a hand, or nod of a head. His mum had already set off for Bingo. Hatty, his sister, nick-named "Princess" because of her golden hair, was busy, too, watching a war movie while slurping a bright orange lolly. Dad was watching the screen and speaking to someone on the phone. But no! George was surprised and pleased when his dad signalled to him.

"What do you want?" said Ivor. Naturally, the enquiry was about food. "What topping?" he yelled, above the TV. So, they were having pizza. A sure sign that Mum was out or they'd be having an Indian.

His father waited. George, thoroughly out-of-sorts, made him wait as long as he dared before listing off, at breakneck speed, an amazing variety of toppings and extras: ham and mushroom, spicy tomato, anchovy, pepperoni, all rounded off with a large chips and Coke. He closed his ears to his father's usual obscenity.

Fleetingly, he wondered about his sister and the word – that word – the word that was beginning to haunt him. Obese. There! He had said it, at least to himself. Princess she might be, but she was

a decidedly fat one. Could it be that she was —
obese? An obese princess! Even he recognised the
anomaly. And then he remembered. If his problem
was fatty tubes, then it made sense that hers was the
same. With time to kill until the pizza arrived,
George slumped comfortably in front of the TV
and rethought his day.

"Dad…" he began hesitantly.

"What?" Ivor Guzell made no effort to control
his irritability. "What do you want?"

"I just wondered…"

"Well, don't bleeding wonder. Get off your arse
and get some cans." He waved an empty one under
George's nose before returning, rumbling and
grumbling to the TV where he used the advertising
breaks to flick over to teletext and check the result
of the 2.30 at Kempton Park.

George closed his mouth and rose to his feet.
There was so much he wanted to know and so few
people to ask.

As they finger-picked through the giant-sized
pizzas, George turned his attention to how he might

occupy the evening hours. He was saved too much worry when his sister, who was flicking through the Radio Times, announced, "*Christmas Carol!* Boring!" As there was still no reaction she added: "We're doing it at school."

Ivor Guzell didn't raise his head from the last of his giant pizza. "Watching it?" There was no pressure there.

A long silence followed while Princess considered the facts. Fact 1: she didn't want to watch it. (Alongside *Big Brother* there was no contest.) Fact 2: she was supposed to have read the paperback by now and hadn't. Fact 3: she was already in big trouble regarding her project. Fact 4: if she watched it now she could claim to have read the book and Miss would never know the difference. Fact 5: was it worth the sacrifice of *Big Brother*? Reluctantly, she conceded that it was. She needed to watch.

"And what am I supposed to do while you're watching that c...?" George was about to say a very rude word but was interrupted by his father.

"George!" shouted his father. "You'll do what you usually do – bugger all! Now stop whinging and watch it or go away and do something else.

And if you've finished with that pizza, pass it over here."

George forced himself to finish the pizza, toppings and all, in an effort to deprive his father, who was clearly still hungry. Then he turned his attention to the polystyrene container of chips which he had been saving as a treat. Stuffing the chips into his mouth, three at a time, kept George busy and glued to his seat as he watched one of the strangest tales about Christmas ever to unfold. "I can't be bothered to move. I'm too tired!" he told himself.

What he didn't want to admit was that, somewhere in this macabre story, he felt the stirrings of familiarity. Whatever the reason, he stayed – and stayed – right to the last moment when, as in most stories, good triumphed over evil.

He was still pondering the tale as he climbed the stairs; still thinking about the ghosts who had visited Scrooge and remembering how Gran had weighed her words when he'd asked if Dad was obese. She was usually so straight-up about every-thing. Other people might twist the facts a bit, but never Gran. There had to be a reason why she hadn't given him a proper answer.

"Is it possible," he asked himself, "that we are all too fat? And that Mr Champion is right and it's not fatty tubes?"

Closing his bedroom door securely, he opened the bottom drawer of the tallboy. Underneath a mountain of vests and pants, he found what he was looking for — chocolate bars, crisps, peanuts. He stuffed a handful of crisps into his mouth and felt better for the fix of fat and salt. The drawer was no secret. His mum called it his "night starvation" drawer and kept it well stocked. Apparently, lots of people suffered from this — waking up in the night and urgently needing something to eat. He left the drawer open while he changed into pyjamas and then made his final choice.

A picture of Scrooge flashed before his eyes — Scrooge and his bowl of gruel. George and his bar of dark brown chocolate. He laughed. He knew which he'd rather have. The house felt strangely quiet. He opened the door, stood out on the corridor and listened. The TV was going full blast but even that seemed rather remote. Hatty's door was shut tight and there was no rustling of sweetie papers or muted PC. He returned to his own room and leaned his back against the door. He shivered, feeling suddenly cold despite the fact that the central heating was working overtime. Clutching the chocolate bar, he collapsed into bed – springs resounding as he hit the mattress. He pulled up the duvet and scoffed most of the bar before falling into a troubled sleep, with the last piece of chocolate clutched tightly in his hot fist, where it began, slowly, to melt onto the white cover.

FOURTH COURSE

The First Spirit

George sat up. Bolt upright! The room was dark except for a fire that glowed in the grate. Strange! George could not recall there ever having been a fire in the grate before. You didn't have fires when you had central heating. The light flickered in odd corners, creating shapes and shadows on ceilings and walls. He lay back to watch. It was oddly cosy and comfortable.

Now that his eyes had grown accustomed to the semi-darkness, he was able, by the light from the fire, to see the room more clearly. "Scrooge's room!" He spoke the words quite loudly. "Yes, that's what it is. It's Scrooge's room." The fact that it was set in more recent times completely escaped him. As did the twentieth century clothes of the man sitting by the fire.

"Are you a ghost?" asked George. His tone suggested it was the most natural thing in the world to wake up and find a spirit sitting by a fire that normally didn't exist.

"Not really," said the man. "But if it makes you more comfortable to see me like that, that's fine. Go ahead."

George nodded. Still unmoved by the strange goings-on in his bedroom, he enquired, conversationally: "So, what do you want?"

"To show you a thing or two. Things you don't seem to want to know. Things it's time you did know." The man stood up and, without any obvious effort, was instantly sitting on the end of George's bed.

"How did you do that?" Far from being scared, George was fascinated. "I never saw you move and yet here you are on my bed."

"Look, if you're going to question everything I do, it's going to be a long night. Just accept that there are some things you're not going to understand. Okay?" Clearly, the man or ghost, or whatever, was on a short fuse.

"Sorry!" George apologised, politely. He was familiar with this sort of treatment. The man gave him a long, hard stare. George felt uncomfortable and tried to look away but something in the man's unwavering gaze made it impossible for George to lower his eyes. But the more he was forced to look, the more familiar the man's face became. Of course! It was Dad! Dad playing a joke. He stretched out a hand to touch the man's arm. There was nothing there. Visibly, the arm was there. Physically, George's hand just passed through it. "Dad?" George faltered. His voice no more than a whisper, he repeated, "Dad!" It had sounded a little like Dad. It looked a bit like him, too. Suddenly, despite the fire, George felt cold, cold with fear. This man sitting on his bed, in the middle of the night, was definitely not his dad. He was thinner, and quite a lot older, more tired and harder – much harder. "What do you want?" George croaked, fear robbing his voice.

"I've already said. To show you something." The boy shivered. Instinctively, he knew he was not about to like the experience.

"And what if I don't want to see what you have to show me?"

The man was looking at him again. Frowning, as if he didn't like what he saw, "Going to bring up the fatty tubes, are we?" he sneered. "I can't believe you're really my great grandson." George started. Great grandson! That made the man old... really old. "Get up!" ordered the man.

"But I'm in bed. It's bedtime." George didn't want to get up. He certainly didn't want anything to do with this grumpy, grouchy old man. So long as he stayed in bed, he felt reasonably safe.

"Bring your mother to see me, will you! Well, go on then." Echoes of yesterday and Mr Champion. George tried to call out and found he couldn't make a sound.

"On your feet, lad." There was something in the voice that said, "And don't muck me about."

George felt his feet swing out but he was not conscious of having given them the order to do so. He began looking for his dressing gown and slippers. There was a distinct chill in the air now. The fire was out. One great swoosh down the chimney and it was gone. "You won't need them," said the man, interpreting the search. "By the look of you, you've enough fat to keep yourself and half the regiment warm."

"Regiment!" repeated George. "What regiment is that? Are you in the Army?"

The man snorted. "Wake up, son. What does this look like?" He patted the khaki battledress. "It's not fancy dress, mate. More's the pity." The last words seemed not to be for George's benefit. More for himself.

"I don't understand what's happening." George resorted to the whinging, whining sound he had perfected over years of practice.

"And you can stop that noise." Eyes, blue as a Norwegian fjord, froze George to the spot. A voice like a sergeant major's rapped out the order, choking the sound in the boy's throat. He had never heard anything like it except on TV in a programme about bad boys in the Army. "Any repeat performance and I'll give you the good hiding your father should have given you years ago."

Good hiding! It was an expression with which George was not familiar but felt that he understood. Give him a good hiding, would he? Well, he'd report him, although he was not quite sure to whom. But he was clear on one point: his great grandfather couldn't get away with that. He'd told his gran as much, earlier, when they were talking about the "good old days." As if reading his thoughts, the man said: "All that modern drivel cuts no ice with me, laddie. In my days, you did as you were told or risked a thrashing if you didn't. As for today," he patted his uniform, "everyone has to learn to pull together, if we are going to end Adolf's little game."

George did some unaccustomed quick thinking. This was the man in the photo on the piano. To him "today" was not necessarily "today's today" but might be "a long-ago yesterday." World War Two. He couldn't remember the date but he knew all about Adolf Hitler. But where were they getting ready to go? Where was Great Grandfather taking him? His mother would play merry hell if she found him missing. He raised these concerns with Great Grandfather but was careful not to whinge.

Again, the man was ahead of him. "She'll never know you're missing. Look!" He pointed towards the bed where a prone George slept, one hand pillowing his head, the other clutching the last bit of chocolate.

"Disgusting!" Great Grandfather looked closer

and inspected the melted chocolate. "You should have lived during rationing. Sweets were a rare luxury. If you were lucky enough to get any, you certainly wouldn't have wasted them mucking up the bedding. You'd have sucked them carefully, trying to make them last as long as possible. Anyway, you'll see what I'm talking about." He held out a shovel of a hand. "Mortimer Guzell. My friends back yonder all call me "Mort". Means death, if you're interested." George cringed. Just his luck to have a great grandfather who enjoyed being called Death. "Anyway, pleased to meet you. Despite the chocolate." His hand, calloused with hard labour, reminded George of cold, slimy seaweed. Presumably, ghosts all felt like that. Man and boy passed effortlessly through the wall of the house. One look at Mort's face stopped George asking an obvious question.

He stifled a scream with difficulty when they reached the street, but he could not hide the fear in his voice, the horror in his eyes or stop his body trembling.

The sky was on fire. Flames licked the sides of buildings. Explosions followed one upon another; a firework spectacular without the variety of colour or cheers of the crowd. Searchlights streaked the night sky looking for enemy planes. Worst of all were the sounds; the intermittent roar of the big guns resounding against the buildings in that narrow, terraced street and the continuous bark of... "Ack-ack" explained Mort. "Anti-aircraft guns. Guaranteed to give Jerry a hard time." He seemed unmoved by the noise and destruction around him. Or was it that, after two years of war, he had schooled himself not to react?

But then George remembered. Today, he and Mort were onlookers. Somehow, though, he thought it unlikely that this man had been any different back in the forties. He reminded himself that he was still George Guzell and that the year was not 1942 but the twenty-first century. Even so, he could not quite control a shiver as the sound and fury of destruction continued.

"And the people?" Suddenly, George wanted to know more. "What about the people?"

"See that?" The man gave him a none-too-gentle push. "See that?" It was a pile of bricks. "That, my son, was a house yesterday. Today it's a pile of rubble. And the folks in there? Dead!" He saw the look on his grandson's face. "It's what happens in wartime."

"Wartime! Wartime!" George repeated. What had all this to do with him?

"Don't keep repeating yourself," Mort snapped.

"It's just that wartime is dangerous!" Even as he spoke the words, George knew how ridiculous he sounded. Again, he had forgotten he was just an onlooker. The pile of rubble made it seem all too real. He felt vulnerable. A target. Part of the noise and destruction.

"Of course, it's bloody dangerous, you clown. Got my ticket D Day."

"So... you're dead."

"Give him a medal!" The soldier spoke to himself. "Of course I'm dead, you idiot. That's why I have come to see you. See if I can show you the error of your ways. Life's just too cushy these days. When I think of the way we lived back in the forties! But we had something! Something, I sometimes wonder, if you and your generation will ever have. Guts! Yes, that's what we had – guts." He gave George a smart shove in the back. "Come on, I'm going to show you what life used to be like. You, sonny, wouldn't have lasted six minutes, never mind six years. And if you ask me, even though it was wartime and, as you say, "dangerous," it was a damned sight more satisfying than what your lot have opted for." George knew he had to be wrong. Wartime couldn't be better. But as he seemed to be in no position to argue or – better still – walk away, he kept his own counsel.

By now, they had reached a small, terraced house, further along the road. There was no sign of life, all the windows blacked out in order not to attract the attention of enemy planes. He noticed the funny patterns all over them. "Sticky paper," his companion informed him, "to stop the glass falling in if a bomb drops close by."

Mort pushed open the door, calling out as he did so. "It's me, Myrtle." Pulling George in beside him, he shut the door before switching on a shaded light which just about illuminated the way through to the back room.

"Hello, luv. Come on. Your tea's ready." Clearly, Myrtle did not see George and he took up the place Grandfather had indicated by the side of the kitchen range. While Myrtle fussed over Mort, he had time to look around. It was a tiny room with a pulley full of freshly ironed clothes hanging from the ceiling. There was a table and four chairs – all dominated by the cooking range with its bright, open fire and mantelpiece full of shiny brass. The floor was covered by linoleum, although George didn't recognise it as such, and made slightly warmer by the addition of a couple of rugs made from scraps of old material and strips of stockings. George had seen something very similar in an old film and had thought it really ugly.

Myrtle was returning from the adjoining room. George risked Great Grandfather's displeasure by moving over to have a look while Myrtle was busy at the range. Although he didn't know its name, the scullery was like one he had seen on TV. There were red tiles on the floor and whitewashed brick walls. In one corner, there was a large, flat sink with a cold water tap, a washtub and something on a stick which he knew was for banging the clothes about. How could Grandfather claim that things were better then than now? Rubbish! He returned to his place by the fire.

"What are we having, Myrtle?" Mort washed his hands and sat down at the table. George could see no sign of food, just a neatly laid table, pretty check cloth and flowered china.

"You'll never guess," Myrtle beamed. "An egg!"

"An egg!" Mort was clearly amazed. He noticed George's mouth fall open and when Myrtle's back was turned, he gestured for him to shut it. A man of limited patience, his irritation with George was clearly visible. "How did you manage that?" asked Mort, laughingly. "Not Black Market, I hope?"

George vaguely remembered Black Market being mentioned in yet another film. Something about it being an illegal way of buying things that were officially rationed. You could go to prison for that. Myrtle gave Mort a playful push. "As if...! You know old Joe, down the allotment? Well, his bantams laid and when he knew you were due home on leave he sent an egg down for you." All this fuss over one egg! thought George. When his mum did eggs (and that wasn't often because it meant getting down a pan), she cooked at least two, and sometimes three, each!

At once, Mort offered. "Share it!" George cracked out laughing. Instinctively, he clapped a hand over his mouth. Fortunately, Myrtle could neither see nor hear him. Grandfather certainly could and he looked far from pleased. But, share an egg! They had to be joking!

"Oh, no!" Myrtle was having none of it. George

saw that neither of them joked. "Old Joe would be mortally offended if he thought I'd had so much as the top off it. As he says, 'It's for a lad who's doing his bit!'" George assumed that meant being a soldier.

Carefully, almost tenderly, Mort transferred the egg to an eggcup, while Myrtle cut thin slices of bread from a dingy looking loaf. "I've saved a bit of butter," she told him.

"You're a wonder!" said Mort. George watched, fascinated, as Myrtle scraped off an infinitesimal amount of fat for the bread. "Two ounces, isn't it?" Mort clearly wanted George to know.

"Yes. Two ounces of butter and six of margarine."

George thought for a minute. Fifty grams of butter! For a week! He could eat that at a sitting and never notice its passing.

What really amazed him was Great Grandfather's delight at the egg. He thanked Myrtle repeatedly and sent messages to Joe but would not touch a bite until Myrtle agreed to share the bread and butter, spreading hers with home-made plum jam from a clip-top jar. The modest meal, sparse by

George's standards, proceeded to the accompaniment of quiet conversation, there being no TV, no DVD, no record player and the only form of communication – the radio – was clearly not to be switched on while Mort and Myrtle were at the table.

They had just finished eating when a loud knocking at the front door had Myrtle scurrying to the kitchen with dirty dishes while Mort's pleased voice could be heard greeting the callers. A few moments later, a couple walked in. "Mary! Bill! Had a feeling you might turn up!" Myrtle removed the coat-like pinafore and kissed the woman. George noticed that the dirty dishes had been stacked on the wooden draining board which stood alongside the stone sink. He also noticed the absence of dishwasher, refrigerator and washing machine. Did the tin bath hanging on the wall mean there was no proper bathroom?

Like a magician extracting a rabbit, Mary withdrew a small, brown paper bag from her shopping basket. "Thought you might need a bit extra with Mort here on leave." Whatever it was, it couldn't have weighed more than a hundred grams.

"Tea," Mort told George. Loud cries of delight

greeted the present. Myrtle produced the tea caddy from over the range and everyone watched while she added the contents of the paper bag to the small quantity of tea already in the tin. The bag was carefully shaken to remove every last leaf and then, clearly understanding what was expected of her, Myrtle went to the larder and returned with a minuscule portion of hard, unappetising-looking cheese, which was greeted with pleased smiles and then transferred to the same bag which had held the tea. For George's benefit, Mort commented: "I bet that bag's been around a bit."

There was some laughter. "Like gold dust, they are. Thanks, Myrtle! It'll be a real treat for Bill to have cheese in his sandwiches." At his enquiring look, Mort explained that Bill had his lunch down the pit where he mined coal.

These people didn't eat enough, as his mother would say, to keep body and soul together, thought George. No wonder they were slim. But how did they manage to do a day's work on so little food?

Conversation was all about the war, the recent bombings and the munitions factory where Mary and Myrtle worked, all accompanied by half serious, half humorous references to "Careless talk costs lives" and "Walls have ears." Eventually, Myrtle made a pot of tea and produced a cake which the assembled group greeted with "Oohs!" and "Aahs!" George wished he could materialise. This was just up his street. "You're a marvel, Myrtle," she was told.

"Hmm. Well, it looks okay, but be careful. Don't go mad. One piece is plenty."

"Liquid paraffin," Mort mouthed at George. George knew the word, mainly in connection with a smelly heater in Gran's greenhouse. He also had a vague memory of someone on the radio mentioning the use of liquid paraffin in wartime cakes. A mental picture of Gran's chocolate cake, which he had wolfed down with scarcely a word of thanks, suddenly came to mind.

After a while, Mort stood up and, making some excuse to the others, signalled to George to follow him. Out on the street the guns were quiet now, but the sky still glowed from fires that would not be put out so easily.

❂❂❂❂❂

The scene changed and, although they were in the same row of houses, the sun shone on neatly-kept privet hedges and freshly painted wooden doors. Gone were the sticky-papered windows and the rubble-filled spaces. Gone, too, was the blackout. Frilly curtains surrounded flower filled windows. Together, he and Great Grandfather passed through the wall into a back room, which had once been the scullery but was now a well-fitted kitchen with hot and cold water, small fridge and a washing machine.

A woman was in the kitchen preparing a meal. George was amazed to see the speed with which she peeled potatoes and popped them into a pan of boiling water and shelled peas straight from the pod – the children all the while pinching the peas and exclaiming at their sweetness. George could not remember ever tasting freshly-grown peas. He had certainly not known that peas could be sweet. Finally, the woman lit the grill, seared some lamb chops before turning down the heat and setting the table. When the meal was ready, a man and the two children came in from the garden, washed hands in the kitchen and settled themselves at the table.

Instinctively, George looked for the TV. Nobody seemed to notice its absence. George beckoned to Mort. "Who are these people? Do I know them?"

"You should. That's your Gran and Grandpa. The boy and girl are your Dad and your Auntie Mabel."

The chat at the table was general – school, work, friends, relations. Everybody took part. Everybody ate and talked. It looked like fun. Nobody criticised the food and when the meal was finished, all the plates were clean. George couldn't help comparing the amount eaten here and the amount consumed by his family and, also, the amount of waste. His own family ate enormously yet still threw away more than this family's entire meal. Pudding was greeted with exclamations of pleasure. Jelly and blancmange! Kids' food! thought George, watching with amazement as Mum, Dad and the two children tucked in. He thought longingly of the cream gateaux he and his family had several times a week. He thought, too, about the appearance of his family compared with this one. They were about three times the size of these people. The meal over, everybody helped clear away and wash up. Then, the man and the children returned to the garden where they played games with a bat and ball.

Later in the evening, everyone went to the sitting room to watch some family TV on a tiny screen surrounded by a large wooden cabinet.

All too soon, Great Grandfather Mort signalled the end of the visit and, suddenly, they were back in George's bedroom. The recumbent George was still sleeping.

"People of my day didn't have the variety of food that you have today," Mort told George, "but they expected it to taste good and to do them good. We had to eat efficiently – we were fighting a war."

"Efficiently?" said a puzzled George.

"Yes, efficiently. Some of the food we needed had to be imported. Ships had to bring it through a continuous blockade of enemy U-boats which sank many of our Merchant Navy. So, food was precious. We had to have enough of it to be healthy but not more than was absolutely necessary, because that would have been a waste of effort, time and lives. In wartime, you have to prioritise. Rationing was the only answer. Taking into account the availability of essential foods, nutritionists came up with a diet which would keep the whole nation healthy. What is interesting is that, after six years of rationing, the nation was fitter and healthier than ever, before or since. People ate less, George, but they ate wisely."

"Wisely?" George questioned. He realised that he had stumbled into a strange, unknown territory and was facing a novel and baffling concept. "What does that mean?"

For the first time, Great Grandfather Mort smiled gently. It was the question he had been hoping to hear. "It means that your intake of food should be linked to your output of energy. In other words, George, the less you exercise, the less you should eat. Otherwise, the excess is stored in your body as fat."

George thought about this. "My family doesn't exercise at all."

"You're all fat," finished Mort. "Exactly! But what you eat is important too. We all need plenty of fresh food – that is, food that has been recently growing, like fruit and vegetables or alive like poultry, fish or meat. And we need some of it every day. Finally, we need to prepare and cook it properly so that the vitamins and minerals are still there. It's a big subject, George. The French have it right. They serve meals with lots of small courses so you have variety and not too much of anything."

George was surprised. He wondered if his mother had been right to stop him going on school trips to France. It sounded quite nice! Grandfather had never mentioned the frogs' legs.

"Well, it's nearly time..." Great Grandfather patted George's arm. "You know, George, it all boils down to respect."

"Respect!" George looked enquiringly at Mort. "What kind of respect?"

"Respect for yourself, your body, your mind. You've got to believe that you're worth something more than a stomach full of junk food. And if that's true – and believe me, George, it is – then the food you eat has to be good enough to be worthy of respect, too. Think about it, son. Respect! Respect! Re-spec..." His voice faded into silence. Then he was gone.

FIFTH COURSE

The Second Spirit

He didn't know how long it had been since Great Grandfather had visited him. Or if there had been any passage of time whatsoever. He thought he had slept. It could have been minutes, it could have been hours. All he really did know was that, as before, he was suddenly wide awake, sitting bolt upright.

But this time was different. This time, he was both excited and terrified at the possibility of yet another adventure. As his eyes grew accustomed to the half-light, he tried to identify the figure at the foot of his bed. George felt a cold chill the like of which he had never experienced before, not even when his great grandfather had taken him into the Blitz.

There, bold as brass, large as life, at the end of George's very own bed was none other than Robert Canterbury Knight – Gruff himself, Headmaster of the Worthington Knight Comprehensive School. It was George's nightmare of nightmares. He whined. He gave it all the whinge factor he could muster. "Sir! Does my mother know you're here?" It was his worst threat. Yet, Mr Knight laughed.

"I'm looking forward to her finding out," chuckled Mr Knight. George nearly fainted. Then Mr Knight seized the duvet and despite the boy's attempt to hold on to it, tugged it out of his grasp and hurled it to the floor.

"Please, sir!" He was whining again. It was what he did best. And as no one had bothered to tell him otherwise, until recently, he had been quite happy to carry on. At least, he now recognised it as a not particularly appealing habit.

"Please, sir. What sir?" said Knight, mimicking the boy, with all the whinging and whining exaggerated.

"Please, sir. It's cold." George tried not to moan.

"I'll give you cold," Mr Knight towered above him like a T Rex with flailing arms. George cowered into his pillow. What had he done to deserve such a visitation? He tried to shout for help but the sound wouldn't come. Only a tiny croak.

The giant arms swept him to the side of the bed and, in one continuous movement, into a standing position. George shook and shivered, not from cold but from pure, unadulterated fear.

"Get these on!" From behind his back, the Head magicked a pile of clothes. They weren't George's. Since when had he ever bothered to wear, let alone own, a tracksuit or the trainers to go with it? "I don't wear this sort of stuff," he sulked.

"You do now," Robert Knight told him. It was then that George noticed the Head's clothes: a well-fitting navy tracksuit teamed up with top-of-the-range trainers. George was amazed. Never, in all the time he had been at school, had he seen the Head in anything other than Headmasterly trousers, jacket and tie. He wanted to make a comment, but something in the Head's eyes suggested that discretion might be a better option. Acknowledging defeat, George struggled to get massive arms and legs into the unfamiliar gear. Fortunately, it seemed to have been tailor-made with him in mind.

The tracksuit was extra large, taking all his bumps and bulges with ease, while the trainers were suitably sized to fit not only the length of his foot, but also to act as support to George's huge ankles and podgy insteps.

This time, there was no friendly handshake, no guidance out of the bedroom – just a school-masterly shove in the right direction. George wondered why it was that spirits were able to push him around while he was quite unable to do the same to them. It didn't seem fair. He stole a back-ward glance at the bed where, as before, his other self lay sleeping.

This time, they went down the stairs past the room where his parents slept, past his sister's room and out by the front door into the street. Was this because the Head, not being dead yet, was not a proper ghost and could not pass through the walls as Mort had done?

As before, they didn't walk or run or fly. One minute, they were outside in the street, the next they were in school, standing in the middle of the gymnasium – not George's favourite place. He was much more comfortable in the adjoining cloak-room where he had happily skived away so many games and gym lessons. Tonight, he was where the action was: the real place with the wall bars, ropes, vaulting horse, mats, beanbags and all the other trappings which George had always taken such care to avoid. A group from George's class was already there, queuing up for turns on the box with the Deputy Head urging them on. George felt a push from behind and found himself standing alongside them. He could feel their breath on his face, smell their hot, sweaty bodies but although they were close to him, nobody saw him. One boy put his hand right through George in order to push another boy – just for fun, of course – but it left George feeling distinctly odd, so odd that he moved himself to the back of the queue. He was not too happy about people poking hands through him as if he were a ghost. He wasn't dead. Well, he didn't think so, not yet. He wanted to get out of there, go home at once but his feet seemed to be rooted to the spot.

One by one, the boys jumped the box and joined the group around Mr Champion. Finally, there was only George left. "I don't have to do this," he began. After all, no one could see or hear him, except Mr Knight.

"Do it," commanded the Headmaster.

Almost in tears now, but physically incapable of disobeying, George started his run. His breath was a series of gasping pants. His steps were too short and too slow. He never achieved anything like enough speed, so there was never the remotest chance that he would launch himself into the air and clear the box. He simply ran straight into it and fell over, banging his head on the corner of the box as he went down, puffing, panting and weeping. Tears rolled down his cheeks while an egg-sized lump developed on the side of his temple. He lay there, unseen. Nobody came. Eventually, half-dazed, he picked himself up and staggered over to the wall, unaware that his classmates were already queuing again for another turn. Suddenly, he realised that all his injuries – the lump on his head and the pain in his body – had vanished!

He heard the Headmaster's snort of disgust. "It's not as if I want to do that stuff," he told Knight, mustering what energy he could to sound defiant.

The Headmaster regarded him, a strange expression on his face. "Are we quite sure about that?" What was he on about? Of course, he was sure.

"Isn't it more a case of telling ourselves we don't want something, simply because we feel we're not up to it?" George was still feeling so sorry for himself that the meaning didn't sink in. "Sour grapes, George!" It was a phrase his gran used all the time. "I hope that you're not going to waste your life by always following the path of least resistance. That is what makes rivers – and people – crooked. The greatest danger for most of us is not that we aim too high and then fail to reach the target, but that we set our targets too low and then hit the bullseye. A person going nowhere can be sure of reaching his destination."

Mr Knight didn't wait for any response but joined the queue of boys himself, marking time by stepping smartly up and down until it was his turn to address the box. It was an unspectacular but efficient performance. He took his run, launched himself into the air, slapped the box with both hands and sailed straight over to land with feet together, all neat and tidy on the other side.

George shrugged. What was all that in aid of? If Gruff was trying to show him up or make him feel ashamed – well he had failed. Without further comment, Robert Knight led the way out of the gym, down the corridor to where Mr Champion stood with a group of boys near the cricket nets. The teacher was going through a long list of names. "Baxter, Castle, Davis, Egerton, Fidler, Guzell…" Loud groans. George frowned.

"Not him, sir! Not him!" George was hurt. What did they mean, not him? It was true there wasn't much he could do, but he was a half-decent bat. Surely, everybody knew that. Surely Mr Champion knew that? "Can't run, sir." They were still talking about him. "No use being able to hit the ball if you can't take the runs, sir." Was Mr Champion agreeing with them? "Have you seen him? He's a pudding in batting pads." Loud roars greeted this witticism. Mr Champion went through the motions of shaking his head but George had the feeling that he didn't disagree. "Last time we tried him," the captain of the cricket team took up the story again, "he hit the ball once. Quite a decent shot. Should have gone for two. He couldn't get his feet off the spot for ages. Run out!" George was careful not to catch the Headmaster's eyes. Mr Champion, meanwhile, was making one or two conciliatory remarks in George's favour. But he gave up in the face of so much opposition.

George turned away, disconsolate. He would have been glad if just one of the boys had really stood up for him. On reflection, he supposed they were right. Last time, it had been a hot day and his legs had refused to budge. Someone had said to him that his legs were like tree-trunks. He looked down. It had seemed a bit hard at the time, but it was true, his thighs and legs were pretty gigantic in a woody kind of way. Oak or ash, maybe... George turned to Mr Knight. "Does it mean, sir, that if I'd been able to run I'd have been picked for the form team?"

"It might," said the Headmaster. "But why bother worrying about it? We all know that you don't really care. You're not interested. If you were, you'd be doing things very differently. Forget it." He pretended not to notice the surprised expression on George's face or the way he sneaked a look back at the nets where individual boys were already limbering up.

Mr Knight stopped any further discussion by taking George's arm and leading him through an outside wall. So! He had got some spectral powers after all.

They were now in a Community Centre. George perked up at the sight of a giggling group of girls. They were all talking, mostly at the same time, and in amongst them was his favourite; the gorgeous Sally Larkin. His ears picked up the sound of his own name: not "George" but "Guzell". More laughter. A girl asked if that was the fat boy who had come to the Centre last week. So they had noticed him! At the time, he had felt somewhat out of it. There had been dancing, table tennis and snooker. He'd always been just too late to get a partner. Whoever he asked had just got fixed up with someone else. All agog to hear what they had to say about him, he moved closer. Sally tossed the long, blonde hair away from her face, and rolled her eyes, expressively. "That fat moron! Do me a favour!" George swallowed. Had somebody suggested she liked him? She was certainly denying it now – emphatically. More likely, he realised, somebody had been suggesting George liked her. Well, she was having none of it. "Have you seen him?" she sneered. Loud groans, baring of teeth and vigorous nodding of heads. "Have you heard him –" shrieks of derision, "puffing and panting? He wheezes for England, worse than my old grandpa and that's saying something." The group fell about, Sally laughing more than anybody. George was hurt and upset. He'd never really thought he stood a chance with somebody as pretty and lively as Sally but, until then, he hadn't realised how much she disliked him. It wasn't fair.

It wasn't his fault he was fat. He'd got fatty tubes. He could still be a nice person, couldn't he? So why couldn't those girls, and especially Sally, see it? The sound of Sally screaming with laughter rang in his ears as they left the building.

"What a pity, George! She's a jolly nice girl!"

George doubted that after some of her remarks. Mr Knight observed the unhappy expression on his pupil's face and fell silent. George wondered if he really deserved to be such an object of ridicule. He longed for someone – anyone – to take his side.

"It would mean giving up a lot of things I like," George muttered, not to anybody in particular, more as if he were thinking aloud.

"True," said Robert Knight. "But don't give it another thought. It's not for you."

And as George looked a bit puzzled, he added, "Remember, we saw that in school today. You told Mr Champion. You prefer to be as you are: fat! Very fat! Obese!"

At the hated word, George opened his mouth to protest. But no matter how hard he tried he couldn't make a sound.

They were on the move again. George stared as they flew effortlessly across the sea. Was this what people called "going abroad"? He'd never been out of the country. Well, he'd been to the Isle of Wight but somebody had told him you couldn't count that even though you went on a ferry. Anyway, it wasn't as if he ever wanted to go anywhere. His mother said they ate frogs in France. He'd seen them hopping around the garden and they were one of the few edibles that he didn't fancy on his plate.

Anyway, he'd got used to waving off the rest of the class on school trips. Nobody ever wanted to sit next to him on the coach and the teacher had to ask for volunteers to take turns. Who wanted to spend a week – even a day – in the company of teachers? And why risk eating weird food you might not like?

The scene had changed. He and Knight were now standing on the edge of a small village.

"Where are we?" he felt obliged to whisper, although by now he was quite used to the fact that no one could see or hear him. It was hot, scorchingly so. His body began to drip perspiration.

"We could be at any one of many places in the world. The problem here is repeated over and over again," the Head told him sadly.

"What problem?" George couldn't see much of a problem. The sun shone. Men, women and children squatted outside huts made of mud and straw. He might not fancy it himself but they looked happy enough. He might have seen something like this in yesterday's Geography lesson.

"Poverty. Shortage of food and water. Something you wouldn't know much about. You always sleep through the lessons immediately after lunch, don't you, George?" (How did he know? He wasn't even in the room.) "It's a case of "I'm alright, Jack!" Mr Knight sounded angry.

"Why don't they do something about it instead of sitting around all day?"

Robert Canterbury Knight appeared to choke. Strangely enough, although he didn't actually speak, George could hear everything the older man thought. "That's rich coming from an oversized layabout like you." The Headmaster itched to give George a clip round the ear.

"They try all sorts of things! And they never stop." The sadness in the man's voice moved the boy.

Contrary to popular opinion, being fat did not

make George insensitive. "So they're really hungry?" He couldn't bear the thought of people actually starving.

"Very hungry, George. Do you see that woman, the one with arms and legs like sticks?" George nodded. "Her job is to fetch water. There are no kitchens or bathrooms. No water on tap. Not even a well, any more. The spring ran dry months ago. Every day, she gets up at first light and walks two hours to bring back as much water as she can carry in that pot balanced on the top of her head." George tried to imagine carrying that much weight on his head. He thought about the way everyone at home took water for granted. Here, it was liquid gold. But Mr Knight was speaking again. "When she gets back, she sets off to do the same journey again. Eight hours out of every day is spent doing just that. Of course, if she had more to eat she would be quicker. Food of the right kind gives you energy..."

But George wasn't listening. He was already half way across the compound where he'd seen a small child lying curled up on the ground – so still, he might have been asleep. Bones starkly formed the child's ribcage and his arms and legs, like the woman's, were just sticks. George looked down at his own huge limbs. And he wanted to hide. "George," said the Head, now standing beside him, but without any of the earlier animosity, "How old do you think he is?"

George thought carefully, taking into account, size, height and posture. "About... three," he faltered.

"Nine!" Knight didn't trouble to explain. The facts were there for George to see.

The boy stepped closer. The child on the ground made no move, no response of any sort, even when George stood right beside him. He just lay, curled up in the foetal position. His shrivelled body was dominated by an over-large head, which had continued to develop even when his body had stopped doing so. Huge brown eyes stared up and through George, seeing neither him nor any of the surroundings. "Why doesn't he do something about the flies?"

"I thought I'd already explained." The Headmaster sounded impatient. "When you don't get enough to eat, you haven't enough energy to do even the most basic things and that includes swatting flies. That child couldn't raise his hand now to feed himself, even if he had the food."

"Is he really going to die?" George thought of the food he and his family wasted on a regular basis. He pictured the overflowing dustbin. He thought of the way his family gorged from morning till night. One tiny piece of pizza would be Christmas to this child. As if reading his mind, Mr Knight said, "Oh, we're all to blame, George, to a lesser or greater degree. Because we don't usually witness this sort of thing at first hand, we're careless with what we have. It doesn't seem to matter that we throw away enough food and drink to feed the world every single day."

"So, what can we do?" George challenged. "Can't we help?"

"There are food programmes, government aid. Short of having a world government to regulate the world's resources, I don't know how you redress the balance. What I do know, George, is that some of us – you included – are killing ourselves by eating far more than we need. It's a sad fact that while we in the West hasten our own death sentence through over-consumption, there are just as many dying in other places because they haven't even the basics to carry on."

George was moved. He'd been moved by the woman and by the child who lay dying on the ground. But the picture that flashed before his eyes was of a piece of dark chocolate that had simply melted away on his duvet. When he thought about his night starvation rations, he felt deeply ashamed. When he recalled how Mr Champion had tried to cajole him into accepting food – anything on the menu so long as it wasn't chips – he felt sick. He remembered his great grandfather and the egg.

"I wish I had something to give him." George's words were addressed to Mr Knight but his eyes never left the tiny boy.

Knight shook his head. "As far as he's concerned, we don't exist. But maybe, George, you will do something – not now, not here – but one day. Come along." He put his hand on the boy's shoulder. "It's time for us to go."

Some time in the next thirty seconds, Robert Canterbury Knight vanished. George found himself back in his bedroom where his body merged with that of the slumbering George, shrouded in his white duvet.

SIXTH COURSE

The Third Spirit

The arrival of a third nocturnal visitor caused George no surprise whatsoever. After the first two, he'd prayed there would be no more. He'd lain in bed with fists clenched, trying to think about anything so long as it had nothing to do with either Great Grandfather or Gruff Knight. And now there was another! George felt he somehow knew the spirit but he couldn't place him. "Don't I know you?"

The man, making no reply, just seized George's hand and pumped it up and down for a few seconds. As with Great Grandfather, it was an odd experience: a much younger hand than Mort's but still with the same cold, slimy feel. "Do I know you from somewhere?" He asked again. This time he got out of bed. He might as well. From past experience, he knew what would happen. He stood barefoot by the side of the bed, waiting for orders.

The spirit just stared at George as though fascinated. Or was he in shock? Whichever it was, his piercing, dark blue eyes never left George. His penetrating gaze compelled George to stare back. He found he couldn't look away even though he wanted to.

The spirit was good-looking, slim, and lightly tanned as if he spent a lot of time in the open air. He had dark brown hair, not unlike George's own. The open-necked black shirt and light grey two-piece suit really appealed to George, who rarely noticed clothes. It would be nice to wear something like that himself in a few years, if he could.

"It's just that there's something familiar about you. I'm sure I know you from somewhere..." George looked into the smiling blue eyes.

"See for yourself," invited the spirit. "Come on! Come closer! Take a good look!" He placed a hand on George's arm turning him – and then himself – towards the long, wall mirror. "There!" The boy's eyes widened. He moved closer. The man stepped closer, too. Both faces almost touched the glass, identical blue eyes looking first at themselves and then at each other.

Ridiculous! George stepped back. So did the spirit. Face to face, they stood within a few centimetres of each other. "I don't understand." George whispered. "It can't be...?"

"Oh, but it is," the man told him. "It's simple. I'm your alter ego."

George frowned. "My alter what?"

"Ego," repeated the spirit. "I'm your alter ego – your other self."

"I still don't get it." George lowered his gaze, confused. "Are you saying there are two of me?"

"Think of it this way," said the other George. "I am another version of you. I am you as you could be in ten years' time, if you want to be. Understand?"

"You can't be! It's impossible!" To prove his point, he tried to turn the other George back to face the mirror but when he put out a hand to grab him, there was nothing there. Obligingly, the spirit turned himself and then the two Georges stared at each other, through the looking glass.

"What do you see?" enquired the spirit.

George gulped. "Two people." He paused to think. "Two people who look a bit like each other." He saw his companion's grimace and apologised at once. "Sorry!" he said. "It's almost as if they're re-lated," persisted George.

The spirit laughed. Like Mr Knight's laugh, it wasn't amused. "Oh, they're related alright. They don't come much more closely related than this. I've just told you. You are the thirteen-year-old George. I am the twenty-three-year-old George *if you want me to be so...*"

George groaned. "You can't be me. I see me and I see you. You don't want to be me. I saw that just now and I don't blame you. You're... well... you're..." He searched for the right word, "nice," he finished lamely. The spirit raised his eyebrows. George tried again. "What I mean is that you're... you're..." he paused still unable to say the word.

"Slim?" the spirit helped him out. Rather cruelly, George thought. "Whereas you – well, not to put too fine a point on it – you're fat." George cringed. "Overweight!" George tried to shrink inside himself. "Obese! Yes, you'd probably be classed as clinically obese."

George swayed to and fro hugging himself in misery. "No! No! Don't say that. Please don't say that," pleaded George. "Not that word. The ooo – ooo – obe…"

"Obese," said the spirit. "Obese! Obese! Obese!" he chanted. George clapped his hands over his ears. The spirit lowered George's hands gently. "It's just a word, George," the spirit told him. "Really easy to say if you're slim, but not so easy if you're fat. I daresay you can force yourself to say it if you give your mind to it. Make the effort, George. You can do it!"

"I don't want to and you can't make me!" There was a hint of a threat in the spirit's eyes at this defiance. "You said yourself that it's not easy, when you're… well…" he hesitated. The spirit fixed him with a compelling stare. "Alright… " George conceded defeat, but it was through clenched teeth. "I'm – not – slim."

"Hallelujah!" cheered the spirit. "At last!" He did a little dance and raised his arms in a gesture of relief. George didn't know what to make of it or why the spirit should be so delighted.

"You know, it's hard work, George, to become obese." George had never heard anyone say that before. Working hard to become fat? That was a new idea! "And, my, how you've worked!" continued the spirit. "Day and night! Night and day! Eating and drinking! Drinking and eating!" George's frown grew even deeper; he knew when he was being mocked. "George Guzell. Eats for England! Wants to eat for the world! Where shall we begin?"

George felt dizzy. His head began to swim and his body to sway, slowly at first, and then faster and faster. At first, George thought he was the one who was moving. But he was wrong. It was the room! Round and round it revolved until George cried out: "Stop it! Someone stop this! I feel sick!"

After a moment or two, the room came to rest. It was no longer the familiar bedroom where George habitually went to sleep, with its PC gleaming in the dark, stacks of CDs and DVDs, pile of dirty clothes and unmade bed... It was a warehouse, shelved from floor to ceiling with every sort of food. George nearly keeled over, faint from pleasure of a kind he'd never experienced before. Nothing much shone here unless it was wrapped in kitchen foil. But as far as George was concerned, this was the Crown Jewels, the Mona Lisa and the wealth of Tutankhamen all rolled into one. Saliva dribbled down his fat chin as he looked and longed. Hands outstretched, he walked towards a shelf lined with biscuits – chocolate, marshmallow, jammy dodgers, custard creams, bourbons... "Give me!" he shouted. "Please, give me!"

Spirit George laughed. "I'll give you, all right. Giving like you've never seen." As if a magic button had been pressed, the shelves began to shudder and shake. George ran from side to side panicking, putting out his hands to hold back the dancing shelves. Any moment now, the jars and bottles might hurl themselves to the ground... Sweets and jams all over the floor. But they all remained in place, rattling and rolling as if they were enjoying the unusual exercise.

Then he noticed that the warehouse seemed to be shrinking. George realised he was at the centre of a moving mass, whose edges were coming towards him. Was it really closing in? He twisted around, looking for an exit. There was none. It was a place without windows or doors. He was trapped in a space that was steadily getting smaller while the shelves full of glorious food were threatening to bury him.

George tried to scream but no sound came out. What had seemed so wonderful, only minutes before, had suddenly become a nightmare.

"Don't look so frightened!" The spirit was back, at last. George had never been so glad to see anyone. "They only want to be near you," the spirit told him. "You should understand that. Aren't you their closest friend?"

"Friend!" George was appalled. "Friends with food?" What was he talking about? "Whoever heard of anyone being friends with food?" he asked. "It's food. I can't make a friend out of food."

"But you have," the spirit informed him. "Best friends, I'd say. Very best friends. You certainly haven't any others that I'm aware of." George couldn't think of any, either.

"Look! Look!" The spirit pointed to a giant-sized pizza which had leapt off the shelf and was even now hovering above George's head. "Sure sign of friendship."

The boy's nostrils quivered. "That's my favourite," he told the spirit. "Sloppy Giuseppi!"

"Mine too," admitted the spirit. "But then, it would be. After all, you're me and I am you."

George perked up. "You like it, too!" This was a whole new and quite exciting experience. It was great to share his passion for food with the good-looking spirit. Things were looking up.

"Yep, it's true I do like the old Guiseppi. It's delicious! But it's only for high days and holidays. After all," Spirit George looked serious, "it's seven hundred and eighty-three calories."

George didn't have any idea what the spirit was talking about and besides, he was too busy trying to capture a portion of pizza as it dodged about above his head.

"Come here!" he shouted. The more he yelled, the more the pizza teased; swooping down quite close and then, just as George's hand shot out, flying away to another part of the room. George wished his legs would leap into the air but, for some reason, they positively refused to budge. Eventually, he gave up on the pizza when his attention had been drawn to a giant pan of sizzling, golden chips. The greasy smell would have knocked out most men and the spirit looked to be struggling. His skin had taken on a greenish tinge. George, meanwhile, was breathing deeply, inhaling that gloriously fatty atmosphere right down into his lungs. He felt he was going to explode with happiness. Chips, at last! The memory of all that unpleasantness at school vanished as the golden sticks came closer and closer.

"Deep fried!" commented the spirit. "None of your low fat, oven baked nonsense here. The real thing! Pity about the two hundred and twenty-five calories, though."

George wished he wouldn't keep mentioning numbers. It wasn't a maths lesson. And while he was thinking this, he'd missed the chips. They were gone! But now, before he had time to lament, "A Bender! A Bender!" he shouted, almost pushing through the spirit in his excitement. He could already taste the bun with egg and chips. Unbelievable!

"Four hundred and ninety calories," intoned the spirit.

George ignored him. He had far more pressing needs. Salivary glands now working overtime, he was leaping around, arms outstretched, as favourite indulgences passed before his eyes but, unfortunately, always just out of reach. "Magnum Double Chocolate!" he screamed. "Wait! Wait!"

"Three hundred and seventy-one calories," chimed the spirit.

"Shut up! Go away!" George roared. "Chicken Korma!" He was dribbling fast.

"Four hundred and fifty-nine." The spirit either hadn't heard him or was pretending to be deaf.

"Bar-B-Q Noodle!" Of all the little snacks, this was George's favourite. It was an extra to be consumed when he was bored – or watching TV – or playing games on the computer – or as soon as he got in from school and, more often than not, when he had just finished a giant take-away and needed a nice finishing touch.

"Four hundred and thirty-three calories," the spirit informed.

"Sausage rolls!" shouted George. There was nothing to beat a sausage roll unless it was two sausage rolls, preferably baked by Mum or Gran. It must be said, however, that it was years since his mum had baked anything. Food came straight from the supermarket, always in a packet and often straight from one freezer to another before it met its ultimate fate in a direct passage to the microwave in Mrs Guzell's kitchen.

"Three hundred and eighty-three calories," the spirit called out.

"Tortilla chips!"

"Four hundred and fifty-nine."

"Crisps!"

"Five hundred and forty-six."

And so it continued; George exclaiming over his favourite foods and the spirit responding with the number of calories for each.

For what seemed like hours, the food frolicked about, flying faster and faster with George puffing and panting as he tried, always unsuccessfully, to snatch a bite. At last, like an exhausted marathon winner who had unwisely opted to run a lap of honour, the boy sank to the floor where he lay curled up, sobbing quietly as he mourned all that he had lost.

At a signal from the spirit, the food disappeared and a silence, broken only by the sound of George's snivelling, heralded the return to normality of George's bedroom.

For a while, the spirit just watched the weeping heap that was his younger self. Then, prodding him gently with the toe of his shoe and waiting for him to open his eyes, the spirit began to talk.

"Let's see…" he looked George up and down. "I'd say about five feet five, 1.65 metres." George neither agreed nor denied. "Large frame. Should weigh between 57.68 and 66 kilograms, between 126 and 145 pounds, roughly 10 stones." George seemed to have drifted off into his own world of continued misery. The spirit gave him a none-too-gentle nudge. "Are you listening?" George didn't reply. It took a sharp dig in the ribs to focus his attention. "You last weighed in at – not 11, not 12, not…"

"Get on with it, can't you…?" grumbled George.

"Ah, so I do have your attention. Very well, then. You weighed in at seventeen and a half stone." But as George didn't seem to be either impressed or even slightly interested, the spirit added, just for good measure: "All that food you've been crying about totted up to a magnificent four thousand, two hundred and nineteen calories. Enough to feed a grown man for two days." George's snort was somewhere between a sob and a snore. It managed to infuriate the spirit who sprang into action. "Right, that's it! Stop snivelling and stand up!" George seemed to be in some doubt so the spirit just stood him up, none too gently. "Pull yourself together. Time to move on."

"As you already know," the spirit continued casually, as they moved through the wall of George's bedroom, "I am you, ten years older. But it's not quite as easy as that. It all depends on you. You must *choose* to be me: I do not choose to be you." George looked confused. "Let me show you what I mean…"

❀❀❀❀❀

It was a house not unlike the one they'd just left, the difference being mostly in décor and furn-ishings as if a few years had passed and fashions had changed. Basically, it was the same, with the usual props to make running a home easy and, as ever, the dominant feature was a giant TV, even larger and slimmer than the one currently gracing the Guzell home. Laptops had taken the place of the bulkier monitors and towers. Generally speaking however, life appeared much the same. The people here were younger than George's parents, yet larger. The same sort of family but a more youthful version.

The colossal couple sat close together on a large, comfortable looking settee. The man had one arm round the woman's shoulder and with the other he was stroking her fat hand. She was crying and he was clearly trying not to cry himself. George turned to the spirit for explanation but he just shook his head indicating that George should concentrate on the couple. A baby cried. It was a miserable sound and the man got up, collected the child from the carrycot and placed her in the woman's arms.

Hugging and rocking, she tried to comfort the child, while her own tears fell on the baby's pink blanket. "How is it possible?" she moaned. "How can it have happened? She's so tiny. She's hardly arrived, and already, it's all gone so wrong. Our own little princess!"

That sounded familiar… George thought about his sister. "What have we done to deserve this? How can God be so cruel?" The woman looked to the man for comfort. He could only shake his head.

"It's not God's fault," muttered the third spirit. "It's yours, you moronic, stupid creatures."

George was appalled. How could he be so unkind? Couldn't he see how cruelly they were suffering? Sympathy was what they needed, not vitriol. He felt ashamed of his other self. "Is the baby ill?" he questioned.

"Oh, yes. She's ill, all right. Diabetes. Ever heard of that, young George?"

George nodded. He knew the word. Mr Champion had made sure he knew it again, yesterday. "Is it serious?"

"Serious? I should say so! We're talking about a baby, George. A tiny baby. Yes, of course it's serious."

"Can't they do anything?" He could see they were both heartbroken because the child was so ill. Surely, it couldn't be their fault.

"Too late now," said the spirit. George frowned. Was he saying that it really was the parents' fault? He was about to challenge the spirit, when the man on the settee answered the woman's question.

"Mum would have said it was all down to fatty tubes. Inherited fatty tubes."

George gave a start. "Who is he?" he demanded from the spirit. "Fatty tubes" rang a particularly loud bell. "Who is he? The fat man on the settee?"

"Oh, that's you. Sorry, I thought you realised. That is you as you will be if you don't choose to change." George looked at the monstrous heap of flesh on the settee and felt himself go cold.

Then he looked round. Where was she? Where was his mum?

"Oh, if it's Mum you're looking for, or Dad, forget it. They've been dead for years..."

"Dead!" George whispered, his eyes widening with horror. "They can't be dead. What happened? Did they have an accident?"

"No!" The spirit appeared to take it in his stride.

"Absolutely predictable. No, they killed themselves."

George felt sick. He couldn't bear the thought that his parents were dead and, worse still, that they'd taken their own lives.

The spirit watched his reaction with some surprise. "Don't take it so badly! When I say they killed themselves, I don't mean they committed suicide. Our parents *ate* themselves to death. 'Overeating' should have been on the death certificates – not heart attacks, strokes, high blood pressure. Those are terms the medics use when they don't want to be too specific. Oh, they died from fatty tubes alright, ones they'd created for themselves by constantly eating fatty, cholesterol-filled foods which clogged up their arteries... But you don't have to be like them, you know, George. You can change if you choose to..."

"And the baby? My baby?" He wanted – felt entitled to – some answers. But even as he asked the question, the spirit began to fade away. George was barely able to hear his final words.

"You can do anything you ought to do. Just make a start..."

The room with the grieving parents became smaller and smaller until it finally disappeared altogether.

SEVENTH COURSE

The Return of the Third Spirit

"Fatty tubes! Fatty tubes! Fatty tubes!" He was still muttering as he woke up in his own bed, early light greying the wintry gloom. Of the night's activity, there was no evidence. Thank goodness for that! He felt the great wave of relief that people always experience when they return from the alarming illusions of the night to the blessed normalities of the day.

He lay back against the pillows, taking it all in. Everything was in place: the dressing gown behind the door; the heap of yesterday's clothes; the PC with the green light still glowing; the table piled with unopened school books – reminders of undone homework. Even the melted chocolate was still there, staining his hand and what had once been a white duvet.

It was seeing the chocolate that reminded him. He remembered going to bed, choosing his bedtime rations and all the while thinking about Scrooge. Scrooge! He turned over on his stomach – never an easy thing to do considering its size – and closed his eyes. He would go back to sleep. Yes, that was the answer... Stop thinking about Scrooge – and those awful spirits.

It was no use. His over-active mind had no intention of letting his under-active body rest. It had all been such a dreadful jumble... But did it mean anything? Or was it simply the result of a weird film seen just before bedtime? Or – disturbing thought – possibly he'd eaten something which didn't *agree* with him? He forced a laugh as he thought about all that mobile food in the dream. Glorious, scrumptious food! His mouth began to water at the memory. But then, something unusual happened, something strange and without precedent. He began to experience a slight feeling of nausea. What had seemed so pleasurable turned into something sickening as his mind dwelt on all that food swirling about together. Chips, pizzas, chocolate, chicken korma, ice cream, biscuits, crisps. Ugh! He wondered if he was going to be ill.

George rolled over onto his back, contemplating the ceiling. Supposing... He let his mind wander...

Just supposing... He looked the length of his body. Well, he tried to. "I can't see my feet," he mused, but then, as if the thought had only just properly registered, he said again: "I can't see my feet!" He was horrified. Desperately, he patted his stomach. Gently, respectfully at first, as if trying to make its acquaintance, but then with increasing impatience, slapping himself sharply, he exerted all his strength in his efforts to make his stomach reduce. But it was having none of it. Years of hard eating had created a dome that now had stature and stamina, a stomach of real substance.

For the first time in his short life, George knew the meaning of envy. All that Scrooge needed to do was change his attitude and immediately he became a benevolent old gentleman who wished everyone a "Merry Christmas" and was much loved in return. Unlike Scrooge, he was about seven stones heavier than he should have been and he lived in a house where being supersized was regarded as normal – even desirable – and where Nora Guzell was in charge of the food arrangements.

Sadly, there would be no miracle conversion for him. The cure, if there was one, couldn't be achieved by the opening of a window, the calling to a boy in the street or the delivering of a prize turkey.

Everything was exactly the same as it had been the day before. If the spirits of the night were to be believed, it would be the same tomorrow and to-morrow and tomorrow. Tears poured down the fat cheeks, rolled down his chin and found a route amongst the folds in his neck. Curling up as best he could, he suffered the real torment of his dilemma, his gross body heaving with the extent of his misery.

"I am you..." George sat up and looked around. He could have sworn he'd heard a familiar voice. "Hello!" he called eagerly. But there was nothing to see. No spirit. No alter ego. Nothing.

"I am you only if you *choose* to be me..." The spirit's words reverberated round the empty room.

George considered the words, slowly weighing each one in turn. So, he did have a choice. He wanted to do a Scrooge: shout his joy from the window. He could be that slim, well-dressed, well-spoken version of himself, or he could continue as he was – the George whose parents would die early and whose children would be sick at birth.

The *choice* was his.

"Come on, George, you lazy layabout. Get out of bed. Now!" This time, there was no mistaking the voice. His mother ripped off the duvet and, giving him a resounding slap on his ample rump, propelled him out of bed and down the corridor to the bathroom.

EIGHTH COURSE

George's New Leaf

Breakfast was a silent meal. Ivor Guzell idled his way through one of the more sensational tabloids, lingering lasciviously over the long limbed lovelies who decorated Page 3, while keeping a watchful eye out for Nora whom, as he knew from experience, was quite likely to put her substantial fist straight through the page to within centimetres of his quivering nostrils.

Everybody else watched Breakfast TV and as usual, the opportunity to communicate was lost. As the huge fried breakfasts were handed round, George couldn't help wondering how many calories there were on each plate. His gorge rose as he looked at the glistening fat. He'd been eating and enjoying his mum's fry-ups for as long as he could remember. Now, they made him feel sick. Anxious not to hurt his mother's feelings and to disguise how little he'd eaten, he sliced up his sausage and pushed everything around. Already, his father and Hatty were eyeing his plate with predatory interest. George made a pretence of looking at his watch and stood up.

Used to the way George normally bolted his breakfast, Nora gasped to see the mountain of food he'd left. It was too much for sister Hatty, too. She stretched across the table and shovelled everything onto her own well-filled platter. "And where do you think you're going?" Nora roared and thumped the table.

"School!" They were a family of few words but leaving a plate of food was a serious matter. Bacon, beans, black pudding and thick pork sausages, all rejected, necessitated an explanation, regardless of Hatty's claiming of the booty.

"School?" she echoed. "What about your breakfast?"

"Not hungry!" George's voice trembled. He wasn't used to taking on his mother.

"Not hungry?" screeched Nora.

"Not hungry?" Ivor Guzell lowered his paper. Hatty put down her knife and fork. All three focused their attention on George. What could be wrong with him? "Explain yourself," his father grunted.

Hatty's sunken little eyes examined his face. "Have you got – a stomach-ache?" she faltered. It was the worst fate she could imagine.

"No!" He spoke more confidently than he felt. "NOT HUNGRY!"

"*Not* hungry!" His father was deeply offended. New ideas can hurt some minds as new shoes can hurt some feet. "You'll eat your breakfast... or... I'll... I'll..." He glared at Hatty's brimming plate.

George eyed him speculatively. Although his father liked to think he threw his weight about, if it meant actually getting his huge frame out of his chair, he didn't bother. Usually, George was glad for his father to take little or no interest, but today was different. He felt like doing a bit of challenging – something along the lines of "You'll do *what*, Dad?" However, such bravado was short-lived as he experienced a strange feeling of sadness for the parents they might have been, in different circumstances. Then Nora propelled herself around the table to where George stood. Her heavy breath, still carrying odours of the garlic bread and take-away Indian she had consumed on the way back from Bingo the night before, spread a suitably homely fragrance. "Are you ill?" Her voice softened. He was still her little George, all seventeen and a half stone of him. "I can write you a note."

Normally, George would have leapt at the offer. He was a past master at feigning a headache or bilious attack upon reaching the edge of the playing field or door of the gymnasium. The mysterious affliction of his right knee and its consequent one-sided limp had never been matched by any of the other skivers who sat on the sidelines or truanted in town. Today, George was not interested in sick notes. He wanted, more than anything, to get away from this house and from his own role in the Guzell family: a fat boy in a fat family eating a fat boy's breakfast. "Got to go," he muttered. "Don't want to be late." He grabbed his satchel and, before his astonished family could respond, he was out of the front door.

Nora sat down suddenly, subjecting all the chair's joints to great stress and causing them to protest with loud squeaks. What was wrong with George and who was responsible? Ivor surreptitiously peeked at his favourite page again but abandoned it, almost at once, to put a comforting hand on Nora's substantial knee. Even the irrepressible Hatty couldn't find a voice. In all his school years, George had never been known to express either an interest in going to school or a concern about being late.

Outside the front door, George adjusted the strap of his satchel and set off to walk. Another first! Normally, he sat at the bus stop to wait. Today, he wanted to walk. He wanted to think. With time for both, he stepped out smartly, noticing what a pleasant day it was, especially for December. The wintry sun cast a golden glow on the branches of the old oaks that lined the way. He breathed deeply of the crisp, cold air but was alarmed to find that, as soon as he reached the small incline approaching school, his breath became laboured. Also, his legs hurt and he had to make frequent stops before arriving at the gates.

One or two of the school wags greeted his early arrival with interest. "Georgy Porgy!" It was the usual greeting, which George ignored. "Lots of pudding! Plenty of pie!" shouted another. "But not much chance of kissing the girls and making them cry, eh?" The previous night's encounter at the

Community Centre flashed before George's eyes. He remembered what Sally Larkin had said and how he'd been a figure of fun for all the girls. He worried that everybody shared their view of him. He bit his lower lip until it hurt.

"Come on, Porky! You might as well make yourself useful." This meant being luggage minder while the other boys played football. Having no desire to take part, he was normally quite happy to fulfil this – or any – function, just to feel included. But not today. Surprised by his refusal, George was well away before the boys had time to think of a response.

He was lucky. The doors were open and he walked in, unchallenged. He needed time to think and plan the next move if, indeed, there was to be one. But there was no time to make decisions. Roll call, assembly and the morning's lessons all passed uneventfully. Nobody really expected him to ask or answer any questions but some members of staff had developed a routine habit of firing the occasional shot in his direction just to prevent him from falling asleep. However, for the first time that he could remember, he experienced a brain that was crystal clear and able to consider the true implications of the choice he had to make.

At lunchtime, he ambled down to the dining hall a few yards behind his classmates – not really one of the group. The only reason they even tolerated his presence was because he'd supplied yesterday's entertainment and they had high hopes that they'd be treated to another "Georgy Special" in the dinner queue today.

From his vantage point on the staff tier, Mr Knight was also aware of feelings of tension. Like everyone else, he watched and waited. So, too, did Mr Champion who now moved to join the Head. Both men anxiously scanned the dinner queue and in particular, George, who to their certain knowledge hadn't spoken a word since he lined up. "What's he doing now?" enquired the Head, as George stepped up to the counter and was speaking to one of the dinner ladies.

"I think he's asking what's on the menu." Champion wished they were closer. After yesterday's fracas, he was anxious not to have any more of the kitchen staff upset. The last thing they wanted was a walk-out of dinner ladies and the subsequent bad publicity for the school.

"And what's he going to be told?"

"Same as yesterday. No chips for him!" The Headmaster gave a slight grunt. "Here we go!" They watched intently as the boy turned away to rejoin the queue. To their surprise, there was no sign of reaction on George's face. He continued to wait his turn and when he reached the serving hatch, chose a slice of Mrs Dulgence's homemade lasagne with a spoonful of peas, and sat down at a table on his own.

"What's going on?" enquired the Head.

"Search me. Lull before the storm?" responded Champion, uneasily.

"My compliments, Jack! Your words of wisdom seem to have done the trick."

Both were smiling with relief. But Champion was not totally convinced. "Thank you, Head-master. Much as I'd like to take the credit, none of this makes much sense. Unless, of course, there are things young George doesn't want his parents to know." They shared another laugh.

Despite their good humour, and quite independently of each other, both of them checked the dining hall and George at regular intervals that lunch hour, each convinced there was something that didn't quite add up. George, completely un-aware of their close scrutiny, had applied himself to his dinner. It wasn't what he was used to, either at home or at school. Slowly, he forced down the lasagne and peas, clearing his plate and conscious that, like the day before, he was still hungry at the end of it.

"Seconds, George?" Mrs Dulgence sensed his lack of satisfaction.

George was in a quandary. He wanted the extra food – was desperate for it – but he was also mindful of the previous night's messages.

"You can have a little more," the cook told him. "It's low fat."

He didn't know what that meant but she seemed to be saying that it was okay, so he accepted another helping, this time eating even more slowly to make it last even longer.

❋❋❋❋❋

It was 'Games' that afternoon. George visited his locker for the first time since the start of the new term. Forcing his arm through a jumble of old exercise books – many bearing the stains of sticky, chocolate caramel and dried Coke – he dragged out a crumpled heap of sports clothing and a pair of trainers. It was a combination that caused the other boys to hold their noses and make unmentionable animal noises. His untidy heap was a sorry sight alongside the regimented piles of crisply-ironed, white shorts, newly-washed jerseys and immaculate footwear.

George was oblivious to any comparison. In a world all his own, he seemed equally unaware of the jeers and gestures which his bloated body provoked as he stripped down to the buff. Donning the grubby, old jersey, he now struggled into excruciatingly uncomfortable, mud-caked shorts. Finally, and because he could find no socks, he thrust his feet directly into trainers that had never been cleaned since the day they were bought.

The other boys were fascinated by the finished effect. Nobody spoke. Some looked as if they might, but didn't. They all sensed the start of trouble. They all anticipated the moment when George would get his come-uppance.

Firm footsteps hurried along the corridor, the changing room doors swung open and Mr Champion strode in. "Good afternoon, gentlemen." Champion always observed the civilities although his use of the word "gentlemen", in this context, might easily have been taken by some as mockery.

The words had barely left his lips before he knew something was up. He was aware that the class were grinning but not speaking. They knew something that he didn't. Not wishing to give them too much self-satisfaction, he permitted himself only a cursory glance around the room. Usual trouble spots were windowpanes, washbasins, coat hooks, and fire hoses... No broken glass. No cracked basin. No foam oozing over parquet floor. Nothing! On full alert now, but not letting his face slip, he turned his attention to the register. The unnerving silence continued. "Notes!" A boy with a broken arm tendered his. Another boy coughed and sniffed his way forward, clutching in his hot, unpleasant, little hand a note that said he needed to stay in and keep warm.

His pen travelled down the list of names. "Guzell! Note!" Not raising his head, he held out his hand for the expected note. The class's collective sharp intake of breath prepared him. So, that was it! Composing his face, he looked up. Every boy's attention was focused upon him. Singled out and with no idea as to the reason, he played for time. "Notes!" he called again. "Guzell! For the last time! Note!"

"Not got one, sir."

He was just about to give him a tongue-lashing when he realised that George was actually dressed and ready to take part. Today, he would have welcomed one of Mrs Guzell's imaginative little notes. "George twisted his ankle this morning and needs to keep his weight off it," was one of her better efforts. What he had not expected was to be faced with this vision of scruffiness. Now he knew why every pair of eyes was turned in his direction. Now, he understood the silence. They were waiting to see how he dealt with this filthy apparition masquerading as a member of the class.

The offence of attending gym in tainted, mildewed, cobwebbed kit was punishable by exclusion from the group and detention. As George usually chose not to attend the group at all, exclusion was unlikely to upset him and over-familiarity with detention had minimised its terrors long ago. If he allowed him to get away with it, he had thirty young vultures waiting to witness such generosity and to take pleasure in attacking their prey – himself –

whenever it suited them.

It was George's face that decided him. What he hadn't noticed before was the sheer misery on the teenager's face.

"Change of plans! We'll do nets." Mr Champion acted swiftly. One or two boys moaned but, for the most part, they seemed happy enough. He handed out the cricket balls.

George declined. "I'd like a bat, sir. It's what I do best..." At the surprised look on Mr Champion's face, he added, "You said so yourself, sir. So did Mr Knight." Champion was non-plussed. He couldn't remember having said anything of the kind.

"And *they* did, too," George continued, looking at the bemused faces around him. "They all said it's what I do best and, if I could run, I might be picked for the team." His face broke into a massive beam of pleasure.

As far as Champion was concerned, George could not bat, bowl, field or keep wicket, so his inability to run was irrelevant and the likelihood of his selection for any cricket team a figment of his imagination. Less enlightened members of the teaching fraternity might have seized the opportunity to ridicule George's delusions of grandeur, condition of kit and rarity of attendance. Champion chose to play along. Obligingly, he handed George a bat and directed him to an astonished group who welcomed him with, "Come on, Porky. Want to bat?" Perhaps, like the teacher, they were curious to see what stunt he might pull next.

Whatever George had in mind, he was incapable of its performance. Arms ached as he struck out at the continuous barrage from experienced bowlers. His legs almost collapsed beneath all that weight. His chest hurt as he laboured to breathe alongside the agony of so much exercise. I can't do it, he thought. He wanted to lie down and let them walk all over him. But he never complained. Not a word, not a look, not a gesture linked him to the misery of that long afternoon. Mr Champion noticed. So did the class. A griping, groaning, grumbling George they all knew well. This new George they knew not at all. So what kept him going? The one thing that George, until that moment, had not known he possessed. Willpower!

Afterwards, in the changing rooms, a couple of boys approached the teacher. "Porky was a bit weird this afternoon, sir."

"Really?" Mr Champion sounded disinterested but was secretly delighted that the boys had also marked George's extraordinary performance. "Well, no doubt time will tell," he commented vaguely, as it gave them something obscure to pass on to the rest of the class. Anxious not to make a wrong move with George, Mr Champion limited himself to a few words of encouragement and a gentle reminder that it might be a good idea to take his kit home and get his mother to give it a long, hot wash in the machine. George, equally anxious not to make a wrong move with Mr Champion, nodded his agreement, leaving Jack Champion thinking along the same lines as Nora Guzell: Kids! You never know where you are with them.

NINTH COURSE

George Explains Himself

By the time George arrived home, his father was already on the phone, ordering a take-away. "Indian, okay?" He waved the phone in the general direction of George, Nora and Hatty but did not wait to consider the grunted responses before returning to his in-depth conversation with Mr Patel at the local curry house.

George didn't know what to do. The little information he'd gleaned from the spirits suggested that the last kind of meal he should be having was a take-away. He wanted to say to somebody, preferably his dad, that he was frightened. But he suspected that if he did, his dad would just give him a strange look, meaning: "Get it down you lad and stop fannying about!" George felt he should be talking to someone, getting advice about calories and diets. He just didn't know where to begin. Was he really one of *this* family? The thought made him feel disloyal. After all, they were *his* – his family – and they loved him. And, something he hadn't ever thought about before, he supposed he loved them too.

Moreover, after a day with no breakfast, no snacks and a small lunch, he was – quite literally – starving. Tomorrow, he'd choose the right food, taking care to get enough of the vegetables and fruit on offer in the hope that they'd fill up all of the spaces normally occupied by chips, chips and more chips. But tonight, his stomach grumbled for a chicken tikka, a large pilau rice, a couple of samosas, two or three onion bhajis and, maybe, a large naan bread. All washed down with a giant Coke. Bliss!

"High days and holidays!" Where had that come from? Oh, yes, the spirit had said he loved an Indian every bit as much as George but that he limited it to "occasionally" rather than "daily." Well, that was a bit of an exaggeration: they didn't have Indian every day. Certainly not! They also had Chinese, Mexican, Thai, pizza, or anything else that came in a container, was delivered to the front door and spared Nora from having to slave over a hot stove before going to work at the local supermarket, where she stacked shelves four nights a week.

Anxiously, George awaited the arrival of his dinner. His rejection of crisps and chocolate-covered nuts caused a few raised eyebrows. By now, the family had decided George was definitely unwell. Indeed, Nora and Ivor exchanged meaningful glances which suggested a visit to the doctor was likely. Not that the local GP's was their favourite calling place. Far from it! What kind of doctor always diagnoses "over-eating" whenever you complain about pains in the stomach or bilious attacks? At the moment, the Guzells were systematically working their way through the local group practice as they searched for a doctor with rather more imagination.

Today's experience had convinced George that he was in pretty poor shape. He had the horrible feeling that he needed to see a doctor but he dreaded the inevitable argument between Mum and the GP which always ended with the family being ordered out of the surgery. In the past, he'd swaggered out through the waiting room, enjoying the startled looks of the other patients who treated doctors like gods. Now, it didn't seem quite so clever. His experience with the spirits had suggested the alarming possibility that other people had opinions too, and that theirs might even be right.

When the food finally arrived, everybody moved in on the long coffee-table situated between easy chairs and the TV and where the ceremonial Opening-of-the-Foil-Containers commenced. Like locusts in a wheat field, they cleared everything in a matter of minutes. Determined to make some sort of effort, George served himself only modest portions, by his standards. Quite deliberately, he ate as slowly as possible, deluding his mother into thinking he was consuming his usual "good meal".

Next day, at breakfast, George said he'd already had his cereal and wanted to get off to school because he'd promised Mr Champion that he'd be there early to set up the gym for the first period. As Nora's washing machine currently contained the unspeakable gym kit, she was reluctantly forced to admit to herself that his excuse might be genuine, "If I find you're lying... " she clipped him smartly round the ear, a foretaste of violence to come.

Of course, he was lying! He scarcely knew how to use the equipment, even less how to set it up. Mr Champion was hardly likely to rely upon him to help. Again, he walked – or waddled – to school.

Head down against the wind and deep in thought, he was surprised to look up and find that Sally Larkin had fallen into step beside him.

"Missed the bus, Porky?" She concentrated on adjusting her quick stride to his slow, ponderous one.

George cringed. Although he'd put up with this nickname for years, he now realised how much he hated it, especially so when used by her. "No!" He kept on walking.

Sally frowned. "But you usually catch the late bus. You always seem to want to be the last person to go into school. Why's that?"

"Oh, I don't know. I suppose the trouble with getting to school on time is that it makes the day so long... Anyway, it's not true. I'm not always the last to get there any more." He refused to look at her. Since that episode in the Community Centre, he'd become more and more embarrassed by his own appearance and never more so than when in the company of the girl he'd most like to impress.

"Why?" Sally's curiosity was persistent. Had George had the ticking off of a lifetime from Jack the Champion? She couldn't think of any other reason why George would walk when he could bus. She checked her watch, twice. He wasn't just on time, either but several minutes early. Very strange!

"Cos I'm fat, that's why!" She stopped, shocked to hear him speak like that. He stopped and his eyes, blazing with fury, met her gaze full on. "Fat! Fat! Fat! Have a good laugh! Why don't you?" He was shouting now.

Sally's face paled. She tightened her lips and swallowed hard. "George!" She trembled.

It was the first time he could ever remember her calling him by his proper name. "What?"

"I'm sorry!" She heard her companion's long, sad sigh and compassion darkened her pretty eyes. "I'm so very sorry... I didn't realise."

"What? Didn't realise I was fat?" All the steam had gone out of him.

"No! No! No! I didn't realise you wanted to do something about it."

"Well, I do. So there! Now you and your stuck-up friends can really have some fun. Just go away." The venom – the self-loathing – had gone. He was tired and overcome by the enormity of the task that faced him. He wanted to be alone.

The girl shook her head. "It's not funny." He stared. "Not funny at all. It's wonderful! Really wonderful, George." She patted his arm tentatively as if she wasn't sure the gesture would be welcomed. "Go for it, George. And... and if there's anything I can do to help..." Her voice trailed away and, still looking slightly unsure of herself, she left him and caught up with a group of girls who'd been giving her some very strange looks.

For George, it was as if the grey, wintry sky had turned blue, the sun had come out and all the birds were singing. The memory of a gentle tap on his arm and Sally's soft words of encouragement stayed with him all the way to school. This time, he even asked if he might be included in the pre-school kick-about, a suggestion which provoked much hilarity and the comment that he might hurt himself – or flatten everybody else.

In terms of football achievement, his kick-about was not a success, although there were two occasions when he nearly made contact with the ball. Later, he spent an agonising morning aching in long forgotten parts of the body while discovering how little he knew about anything. His questions in class were ridiculed by the rest as "childish," the points having been covered by everybody else months ago. Even the staff, initially cheered by his unexpected input, wished he'd go back to his normal soporific state, so the progress of the rest could be resumed.

At last it was lunch time. George was first out of the classroom, anxious to know what Mrs Dulgence was offering. He saw that Mr Knight and Mr Champion were in the dining hall again but George was focused only on getting to the front of the queue. Noticing George at precisely the same moment, the concern of one was mirrored by the concern of the other.

"What *is* the matter with that boy?" demanded the Head. "Look at him, Jack. The Guzell boy! He's a picture of misery."

Quickly, Champion described the events of the previous afternoon.

"Shall I have words? You know, my fatherly figure mode," said the Head. "Something's upset him."

His Deputy hesitated. "Not sure it will do any good. He's in a strange frame of mind."

Mr Knight smiled to himself. He knew his Deputy hated to admit defeat, so he rarely overrode him. "If it's parental trouble, it might be necessary," he persisted. "Keep it out of the classroom domain." His Deputy nodded at once. The Head was right. It was impossible to keep track of all the domestic unhappiness which might upset a child and plunge it into deep melancholy. "Ask him to pay me a visit, Jack. My office. Any time after two."

George was alarmed to get a message to present himself at the Headmaster's office after two o'clock. Although he was glad to be excused Maths, he was far from happy at being singled out by Mr Knight. The Head's room, ideally situated on the first floor between the "up" and the "down" stairways, enabled him to watch hundreds of pupils tramping to and from their lessons and to catch any noisy troublemakers on the way. One red-faced, cocky little second year was just leaving the room, taking care not to meet George's interested gaze.

"Come along, George." The Head switched roles with the ease of long experience. "No need for you to look so worried. Just wanted a little chat. Please sit down!"

Mr Knight watched as George tried to fit his bulk comfortably into the narrow wooden chair. Eventually, George raised his eyes. For a long moment they just stared – man and boy, teacher and pupil – with neither having the first idea what was going on in the other's head.

Mr Knight took the lead. "Mr Champion and I are a bit concerned about the way you've been looking recently. You seem depressed. Is this a school matter or something at home? Is it physical or spiritual, would you say?"

George was amazed. At last, somebody who actually understood. "Spiritual, sir. Yes, that's it, spiritual." His mild surprise at the speed with which Mr Knight had reached the heart of the matter reminded George that the Headmaster had been the second of the nocturnal visitors.

Mr Knight had regretted his use of the word as soon as he had uttered it. What was he thinking of? You don't talk to thirteen-year-olds about things spiritual, not unless they ask you a direct question. George was now looking directly at the Head.

In fact, Mr Knight could have sworn he was staring at his stomach. Slightly embarrassed, the Head shifted his legs. "Getting less, sir?" He was pleased to see the Head's progress. He just wished he could make some himself.

It was so outrageous a comment for anyone – let alone a pupil – to make, that Knight just sat, transfixed. Surely, he'd misheard! Indeed, so disturbed was he that he wondered, fleetingly, if he might be having his own personal breakdown. "It's really working, sir." George looked again more closely this time and his gaze was definitely directed to the Headmaster's stomach. George nodded approvingly. He was beginning to enjoy himself. He stretched out his legs and gave Mr Knight the benefit of a beaming smile.

"What is?"

"Vaulting, sir."

George was surprised when Mr Knight stood up. "Excuse me for a moment, George. I've just remembered something important that has to be done immediately. Don't move. Back in a minute!" He rushed out of the room, sharply shutting behind him the glass door through which George could see him steadying himself.

"Headmaster!" Janet Scripps, his secretary, had never seen her boss so agitated. "Can I do anything?"

But Knight was gone. He strode down the corridor and into the Deputy's room, without a knock or by-your-leave... "Jack!"

His Deputy was on the mobile. "Have to go, love. Robert's just come in... Headmaster?"

"Jack, I think young George is having some sort of breakdown. In my office!"

"Really, Robert? Are you sure?"

"Of course I'm *not* bloody sure!"

Champion looked at the Head's unusually flustered face. "You'd better sit down and tell me what happened."

Knight flopped into the nearest chair. "I hardly know. But one thing I do know – it's not normal for a pupil to come up to the Headmaster's room and make personal comments about his stomach."

"George's stomach...?" Champion spoke the

words slowly, wanting to be quite sure he fully understood.

"No, Jack. Get a grip, for God's sake, man. *My* stomach! *My* stomach!" The Head patted the slightly rounded extension of his waist. "He actually complimented me on getting it down a bit. Cheeky young devil! 'Vaulting,' he said."

Champion rubbed his eyes. It had been a long morning. But glad to have something to talk about less embarrassing than the Head's paunch, from which he now averted his eyes, he said: "If you'll forgive my saying so, sir, I can't recall your taking part in any after school activities in the gym."

"Precisely, man! Precisely! Look, Jack, I want you to come into Janet's office. I'll leave the door of my room partially open and I want you to listen to what young George has to say."

Together, they returned to the outer office and, motioning to Janet to keep quiet, Champion took up his position outside Knight's door while the Head resumed his seat opposite George. "Sorry about that, George. Now, where were we? You were saying about my prowess on the box…" He hoped he didn't hear a stifled snort from the other side of the door.

"Yes, sir." George was delighted. "You showed me, the other night." He saw that Mr Knight was looking distinctly worried. Why? He'd been there.

"Did I, indeed? And where might that have been?"

"It was after you collected me from my bedroom." George had once seen a boy faint. Came to school without having any breakfast, they said. Perhaps Mr Knight hadn't eaten his dinner. He looked a pasty sort of colour. Was he going to faint?

The sound of typing from the next room had stopped. Now, you could have dropped a pin in either room and heard it in the other. Jack Champion looked horrified. "We went to the gym together." Both men were now listening intently. It was no longer funny. A man's career might rest on the way this particular story was told. George sensed nothing of the high drama being played out around him. "It was then," he warmed to his theme, "that I found out that if only I could run between the wickets, I'd be picked for the team." It was lovely to talk to someone who knew what you were talking about. Why did Mr Knight keep frowning?

"And who told you that – about running between the wickets?" enquired the Head, warily.

"The rest of the team. You were there, sir. Don't you remember?" George looked a bit disappointed. "You heard them saying it was a pity I was such a poor runner."

The Headmaster stood up and his tall figure towered over George. "George! Listen to me very carefully. I have never been in your bedroom. I have never been in your house. Never! Not once! Not ever! Do you hear me?"

"But, sir!" George was no longer smiling now. Things were not going the way he'd expected. It was almost as if the Headmaster thought he was lying.

"As for vaulting!" continued Mr Knight, returning to his chair and sitting down. "Vaulting over a box at my time of life is not an option, George. Do you hear me? Do you understand? I don't know where all this is coming from." He was struggling to keep his temper. "It was never much of an option when I was your age, either. I did PE and Games, of course, but I was a very ordinary performer." He looked at the overhanging figure of the boy on the other side of the desk and managed a smile. "As I expect you are. Nothing special. Just an ordinary member of the class." He managed another feeble smile in an attempt to bridge the enormous gulf between them.

"I'm not even that, sir," George hastened to assure him before he added, "You saw it yourself, how I ran into the box. That's why you showed me. But don't worry, sir. Nobody else saw you." He smiled, comfortingly.

Mr Knight thought he was going to be sick. "Are you alright, sir? You're not going to be sick!"

Knight shook his head, vigorously now, from side to side. Mr Champion had his ear so close to the door it was a wonder it didn't swing open. "They didn't see me, George, because I wasn't there."

George adopted that mulish look so popular with teenage boys who believe they're being told nonsense. Knight prayed that Champion hadn't had a class to go to and was still there, monitoring what was going on. He need not have worried. As soon as he'd realised the seriousness of what was being said, Jack had despatched Janet to sort out his classes. A phone call in the corridor and she was back with him, both of them agonising for a boss for whom they shared so much respect. "Look, George, you clearly think I was there." George nodded. "I assure you, I wasn't. Between us, we have to find out why you believe I was. Think about it. What would your mother say if I were to turn up at your house, in your bedroom? She'd have something to say, I'm sure."

George cracked out laughing. "Don't you remember, sir? You said you were looking forward to her finding out." There was definitely a snort from the other side of the door.

Never in a million years, thought Knight, would I take on that woman single-handed and boast about it. He began to relax. "Is it possible, George, that all this about the team and the vaulting is part of a vivid dream? Perhaps you might rather call it a nightmare. I think it's pretty nightmarish to have one's Headmaster invade your sleep as well as your waking hours."

George was deeply offended. "Dream, sir? No, sir. Not really a dream, sir. The spirits were real. Like you said – spiritual!"

"Ah!" said the Head. "Spiritual, indeed!"

"Great Grandfather was first." George was really excited now. "You were second. My alter ego came third." Mr Knight's eyebrows shot up. Latin! Whatever next?

"Alter ego," mused the Headmaster. "Then, we must certainly take this seriously. Was there any particular message from these spirits? I count myself amongst the trio. Am I right?" enquired the Head, outwardly serious but, inwardly, laughing with relief.

"That's it, sir. You all said the same. I'm o-o-obese." George's eyes filled with tears. "Everybody says so." He searched for a grubby handkerchief. Mr Knight proffered a box of tissues and waited while George blew his nose loudly.

The Headmaster was no longer laughing, not even silently. Nor was his Deputy who quietly shut the communicating door and returned to his office. There were some things too delicate for an audience. He knew the Head would bring him up to speed and, now that Knight was in command of the situation, Champion was confident that its conclusion would be a wise one.

"So… What do you want to do about it?" He felt guilty that he must have been giving out some pretty powerful messages to feature in such a nightmare. He moved from his side of the desk to draw up a chair and sit beside George. He repeated his question softly. "So, what do you think you should be doing?"

There was silence. George swallowed hard, wiped his eyes and looked directly at Mr Knight. "That's just it, sir. I don't know what to do. Look at me, sir." The Head did so, greatly to his credit, without flinching. "I'm a mess. I'm not just fat. Not just overweight. I'm obese. The worst fat of all." He sighed a gargantuan sigh of relief as he put it into words.

The Head nodded. He had no intention of pretending. Everything the boy had said was true. The reason the school had gone along with Del Dingley was to try to reverse the national trend which was moving towards an outrageously high percentage of the population being obese within the next five years. Even so, the man's heart went out to the boy. "Have you spoken to your parents?" he enquired. "Surely, they are the people to help you."

George stared. Was he having a laugh? He saw the Head was deadly serious. He wished he *could* speak to his parents. "You've seen them, sir?"

The Head took refuge in: "Not for some time. But they're the people to help you. You must give them the chance."

George couldn't think of one good reason why he should. "They won't like it if I tell them what the spirits say I've got to do... And they'll like it even less if I tell them what you say." Mr Knight now felt distinctly worried. "My dad says: it's a Nanny state and the Government is always telling us what to do and what not to do. And that when we're in our own homes we don't need a load of bleeding do-gooders telling us what not to eat."

Knight let the word pass without comment. "Mind you..." George spoke slowly, his voice little more than a whisper. "My parents won't be around much longer to do anything, anyway."

Mr Knight's face shadowed. "You mean... They're both ill... terminally ill?" No wonder George was in such a state.

"Terminally…" mused George. "Not too sure about that, sir. But they're definitely ill. They'll die long before they should. That's what the spirit said. You know, the other George. They'll never see my children because overeating will kill them." He stopped. And then remembered. "Oh yes, there's the baby. It'll die, too."

"What baby is this, George?" Mr Knight hadn't heard of any such recent event at the Guzells.

"My baby, sir."

Mr Knight felt that reality had slipped away again. Just as he thought they were getting onto firmer territory, George had introduced a baby into the reckoning. Deep mud threatened. Tentatively, he enquired: "Is there something else you should be telling me, George?" No wonder the boy looked depressed. Obesity *and* fatherhood? What a combination! "I didn't know you had a girl friend…" Who was the luckless girl? Was George facing a paternity suit and criminal charges?

"I don't have one. Who'd want me? They made that quite clear the other night, if you remember."

Oh, not that again! thought Mr Knight.

Why does he keep talking about the dreams as if they actually happened?

"And the baby…" continued George. "It's my baby, but in the future." Mr Knight gave thanks for small mercies. But George was explaining. "Diabetes. Two fat parents. It's a bit like Scrooge's Christmas yet to come."

"Scrooge? Scrooge?" The Head suddenly felt the pieces falling into place. He'd seen the TV trailer himself. Now he understood where all this was coming from.

George stared. What did Mr Knight think he'd been talking about? Teachers can be surprisingly thick at times.

"The difference is, sir, when Scrooge woke up, everything was okay because all he needed to do was change his attitude." George's face crumpled again. Mr Knight watched, fascinated. "It's not okay for me, is it? You don't wake up and suddenly become slim, because you can't. No matter how much you want to be. I don't know what to do. I don't want to die. I don't want my Mum and Dad and Princess to die. I don't want my baby to die." Tears coursed down his checks again as he sobbed

his heart out. Janet, hearing the sound, put an enquiring head round the door. In her hand was a
glass of water. A shake of Knight's head and a
wave of his hand returned her to her desk. Perhaps
this was all part of the therapy, she thought.

When at last the sobbing ceased, the Head gave
George a reassuring smile. "There are better times
ahead, George, and I promise that we'll help you.
Yesterday, I was most pleased to hear that you've
already demonstrated a desire to change – to take a
more active part in school life and also, to try the
new dinner menu. Splendid! Well done!" George
smiled, reluctantly. "Before you did that, George,
you were alone and going nowhere. Now you have
a plan. Excellent!" George nodded his agreement.
"So, make the effort and you will succeed. Be a
doer, not a dreamer. Actions really do speak louder
than words. We'll come up with some ideas, I
promise you." Privately, he had no idea what.

'Actions speak louder than words'. 'Be a doer
not a dreamer'. George, his mind full of Knight's
promises, returned to class, where he confounded
the Maths teacher by actually knowing the correct
answer to thirteen times nine.

Back in his office, Mr Knight was less optim-
istic. As George himself had said, there were no
quick, easy solutions achievable by a simple change
of attitude. He hoped that he'd lightened George's
emotional load somewhat but there was still the
physical load of about seven and a half stones of
surplus flab. Only one person could dispose of that
– George himself.

TENTH COURSE

The Visit

Strengthened by his chat with the Headmaster, George passed an uneventful evening at home. He surprised his father by asking for a plain cheese and tomato pizza without extra topping and, immediately after eating it, surprised him even more by going out for a walk.

"A walk!" exclaimed his father. "We don't do walks."

George thought quickly. "Fresh air!" he offered. "It's a bit stuffy in here."

Mr Guzell pondered. "We don't do much of that either, come to think about it." Any further chat was pre-empted by the start of one of Ivor's favourite TV programmes, thus allowing George to slip out and back before his father had properly noticed his absence.

Although he'd not made any real progress on the diet front, the chat with Mr Knight had encouraged him to look ahead. At the same time, Mr Knight was discussing the matter with his Deputy: Why and how had George become the way he was? Whose fault was it? Parents, school, governments and food manufacturers were all candidates for criticism. But Knight and Champion were in complete agreement that George had been failed by his nearest and dearest – his parents – both in the inadequate diet they'd provided and the poor example they'd set.

Talking to the Guzell parents had to be top of the agenda. Neither man fancied the job. Stories were rife in the staffroom about their odd behaviour on the rare occasions when they'd ventured into the school. One teacher described them as "terrifying," especially Nora who was reputed to have "fast hands" and had been prevented from blacking the eye of a teacher, on one occasion, only by the intervention of the caretaker.

"There's a grandmother, I believe," Mr Champion suggested.

"Dodgy!" The Head grimaced. "Parents have every right to kick up if they think we're going behind their backs, even within their own families. Even the Guzells. Let's leave Granny out of it. For now."

Next day, George was stopped in the corridor by the Headmaster. If anything, the boy looked worse than the day before. Crying had swollen and almost closed his eyes, and the dark circles beneath them created a weird, clown-like effect. "I've arranged to see your parents, tonight, George," the Headmaster announced, triumphantly. It had not been the friendliest of telephone conversations but Knight had absolute confidence in his powers of persuasion. "Make yourself scarce if you don't want to be there when I'm there," suggested the Headmaster.

"You won't get very far." The boy spoke with the confidence of thirteen years' Guzell Family History.

Mr Knight threw back his head and laughed. "We'll see about that, young man. You might be surprised."

You might be, too, thought George. Although there are few parents who could be called a "legend in her own lifetime", his mother was such a woman.

That afternoon, George left school promptly and caught an early bus through the estate to the Guzells' wide, end-of-terrace house. As he approached his home from the bus stop, he looked at the house with new eyes, trying to see it as Mr Knight would see it. All the other houses looked neat and clean while the front gardens, although small, were pretty with green and red-berried solanum, dark red cyclamen and winter flowering pansies. Only the Guzell house was different. No shrubs or flowers coloured that late winter's afternoon. A scrubby looking lawn remained unloved whilst the front door looked as if it had never experienced a lick of paint or a rub of brass polish.

If George had been older, he'd have recognised it as the kind of house that usually meant one of two things: owners who were either very poor and struggling to make ends meet or academics whose lives were so book-bound, they never saw the jobs that needed to be done. In truth, the Guzell household belonged in neither category.

Down the open side-passage, George spotted a dustbin brimming over with large flat, white boxes. He didn't need to be the Old Bill to recognise the spoor of the local pizza parlour. The smell of dried, fried onion was a good clue. George, now very much aware that the bin looked both nasty and unhealthy, pressed the contents down with his hand, grimacing as he felt the slimy, cold anchovies against his skin and tomato sauce brush his blazer sleeve. Ramming the bin-lid down as hard as he could, he hoped his efforts would be enough to stop Mr Knight seeing the disgusting pile of empty food containers. He wondered, for the first time, just why his family ate so much junk food.

The house was unusually quiet. Dad was having a snooze, and Mum a quiet fag outside the back door. As soon as she heard the sound of his footsteps, she came in. "What do you mean, you little bleeder, sending that jumped up Knight round here?"

"I didn't." George had no intention of admitting to the meeting in Knight's office the previous day. "He just decided to come."

"So what have you been up to?" Nora frowned. "If you've done wrong, don't look here for no help."

Wisely, George ignored this and went through to the sitting room, from where he could see his father opening the front door to Mr Knight.

"Good evening, Mr Guzell." Robert Knight assumed his warmest smile and held out his hand.

George cringed. His father didn't do greeting so he wasn't surprised when he simply turned on his heel and led the way down the hall back to the sitting room.

"Good evening, George." Mr Knight had spotted him standing at the far end of the room where he was trying to make himself invisible by blending into the door which led into the kitchen.

"Sir!" replied George.

Ivor Guzell extended a limp hand then, stabbing a finger towards the sofa, resumed his own place in front of the giant TV screen. Coloured images dominated every corner of the room while sound blasted out the fact that this was the time of night for *The Simpsons.*

George was appalled. Living with him every day, he'd never fully appreciated how spectacularly rude his father normally was. To his amazement,

Mr Knight did as he was ordered and sat down on the sofa. There was no move to reduce the volume of the television and Knight realised that all the chairs, including his own, were positioned to give maximum access to the big screen. From where he sat, he had a panoramic view of Marge Simpson hectoring the unfortunate Homer.

"Tea?" Ivor Guzell roared the invitation above the sound.

"Thank you!" Although Mr Knight didn't really want a cup, it seemed sensible to accept any goodwill that might be offered. He tried not to wince as Guzell bellowed the order to Nora, out in the kitchen.

An answering roar from the kitchen enquired: "Milk and sugar?" Until that moment, Mr Knight had never thought it possible for anyone to hit so many decibels. Anxious to protect his eardrums, he just nodded his acceptance. Normally, he took only milk.

George watched all of this in fascinated horror. He remembered the neat little tray in the Head's study, with its tiny patterned cloth, fine china and rich tea biscuits.

The two men sat in silence until the tea arrived. One mug was plonked down in front of Ivor Guzell, the other was thrust, scalding hot, straight into Robert Knight's hand. Willing himself not to flinch, he reached for his handkerchief, partly to protect himself from the heat but also, surreptitiously, to wipe the base of the beaker before it dribbled all over his newly cleaned, dark grey flannels. Mr Knight made noises of gratitude for the tea and, under the watchful gaze of Nora, tentatively sipped the dark brew. "Most kind," he said, trying to hide his surprise that Nora, for all her shouting and despite the continued presence of the teabag, had produced one of the best cups of tea he had ever tasted. "And very good!"

George perked up, proud of his mum's tea making. His mother and father nodded to each other, also pleased with the compliment. So far, so good. His dad shoved an upholstered footstool across to George's mum before appropriating another stool by dragging it towards himself, big toes acting as pincers. Both settled back with their large mugs of tea and prepared to watch the rest of the programme. Knight realised that, in this household, the only way to focus their attention would be to stand in front of the TV.

George stifled a groan. "Shall I switch the sound down?" George's voice was not much more than a whisper but the mountain of a man, who was his father, heard. The look that passed between them was clear and to the point. George hung his head, not wishing to meet Mr Knight's eyes.

A child came into the room and sat down beside her mother. Both parents came to life. Knight saw the light in Ivor's eyes and the affectionate way Nora stroked the girl's hair with one hand while feeding her chocolate Smarties with the other. "This is Hatty... Princess!" George told him, with pride.

Robert Knight felt sick. The sight of this huge (little) girl with a quite beautiful face and enormous shapeless body almost moved him to tears. He wasn't quite quick enough to hide his feelings from George who realised that, far from being impressed, the Headmaster was distressed at the sight of the overweight Hatty.

For George, the whole experience was not unlike the events of the recent evenings when he encountered the spirits. Bizarre! Strange! Grotesque! He saw Mr Knight looking at the piles of DVDs which decorated the carpet behind the TV or lay in loose heaps in open boxes near his feet. He saw that his dad had stopped watching the TV and was watching Mr Knight. "Sorry about the mess!" said Ivor. George stared. Since when had his dad noticed mess? But Ivor Guzell was lumbering to his feet. "I'll move this lot out of your way." Making an awkward lunge at the containers, one or two of the DVDs – recordings of the latest Hollywood blockbuster *Web Wonderman* – fell out on the floor.

"Let me." Mr Knight bent down, retrieved them and courteously handed them to Mr Guzell who shoved them back into the box and, muttering something about keeping them for a friend, waddled out of the room. George stared after him. Strange, Dad looking after DVDs for a friend. What friend would that be, mused George.

Knight turned his attention to the room while *The Simpsons* ran on and on. George noticed this and wondered if perhaps the Head didn't like *The Simpsons.* Knight noted all the latest technology and gadgets but there was no trace of a book, no picture or painting decorated the drab walls. Music, literature and art all seemed to be absent. As George had no experience of any of these things, he neither missed them nor wanted them.

Knight wondered if, perhaps, their burgers were their Beethoven and their chips were their Chekhov.

"Sir?" George brought him to with a start. The mugs had been collected and finally the TV stood, sullen and silent! Four pairs of eyes stared at Knight, stared and waited. Mr Knight now found he'd been promoted to top of the bill.

"It's very good of you to see me," he began, diplomatically. "I believe that if we put our heads together we may be able to solve a problem that young George is experiencing at the present moment." George closed his eyes and tried very hard to become invisible.

"What problem might that be?" Mr Guzell spoke for all of them. George saw the tension in his father's unkempt neck, the way Nora's swollen fingers were clasped tightly together. George wondered if maybe they *did* care that he had a problem.

"He's afraid he's too fat," volunteered Mr Knight. George was grateful that he hadn't used the word "obese". Mr Knight regretted that he hadn't.

"Rubbish!" Mrs Guzell lowered her feet to the floor and repeated the word. "Rubbish!" – only closer to Mr Knight this time. Her articulation was excellent. George held his breath. Please, don't let her hit him! he thought.

"Aye! Rubbish!" Mr Guzell took up the theme, though less strenuously. Hatty didn't take up anything. Her teeth were stuck together with chocolate caramels. George gulped and tried to continue holding his breath.

"Puppy fat!" Mrs Guzell was leaning ever closer. "We've all been there!" Her look challenged Knight to deny it.

But even as he considered this delicate point, she switched attention to her husband. The looks they exchanged were conspiratorial. Puppy fat was something they remembered fondly from their teens. "He'll get over it!" She dismissed it summarily. "We all did!"

We're lost before we've begun, thought Robert Knight. But George piped up bravely, "That's not true! You didn't get over it! I haven't! Hatty won't!" He felt a clip round the ear and his mother's strong arms shoved him out of the room.

"Some of us didn't," replied Knight. "George could be one of those. I think he needs help." Secretly, he was disgusted with himself for letting them think he saw George as the victim of puppy fat. Later, he excused it as his attempt to keep the parents on side. George, just outside the door, his ear still smarting, listened to the response.

"Help?" The couple spoke as one. Their voices rose. "What kind of help?" There was no mistaking the awful fear that "help" might mean getting off their fat bottoms sooner or later.

"Diet!" George noted a strangulated quality had entered Mr Knight's voice. He seemed to have lost the ability to have a normal conversation and was resorting to the same one-word communication that the Guzells enjoyed. Eagerly, George awaited their helpful reply.

Perhaps it had something to do with the way Mrs Guzell rose to the bait, every curve, every layer of her fat, flabby body wobbling with fury as she advanced upon Mr Knight. "He's on a diet!" she screamed. George opened the adjoining door ever so gently. He could see his mother hovering over Mr Knight, her beady black eyes flashing, as he tried to shrink his six-foot frame into the furthest

corner of the settee. At any other time, George
would have laughed. Today, horror-stricken, he just
stared, transfixed as his mother's mountainous,
heaving breasts filled Mr Knight's vision and her
breath drowned him in the strangely mixed odour
of tea, mint chocolates and stale onions.

"Diet?" she spat, saliva sprinkling his jacket.
"He's already on a diet. The same bloody diet
we're all on. And a good, healthy diet it is." Silently,
George closed the door. As he had predicted – the
visit had been a complete waste of time.

❂❂❂❂❂

Robert Canterbury Knight, totally crestfallen,
walked back to the school the long way. Pride goeth
before a fall, he thought. He'd failed to make
George's parents understand either the extent of
George's problem or the degree of his misery. He'd
failed to make them aware that the whole family
shared the same problem. On his way there, he'd
considered telling them about the spirits but five
minutes in their company had convinced him that
the spirits would long have to remain George's
secret.

Nora Guzell had, it was true, finally conceded: "He can eat what he likes. But he'll have to see to it for himself. If he's too fussy to eat what's in front of him, don't expect me to make different meals. Too much to do!"

Could this woman be serious? It took every ounce of self-control for Mr Knight to bite back the angry retort that if she'd prepared properly balanced meals in the first place, this problem would never have arisen. So long as George did his own shopping and prepared his own meals, they were prepared to let him get on with it. Fair enough if George had been an adult but, as Knight knew very well, thirteen-year-old boys are not enthusiastic cooks. Moreover, what *could* George actually cook? George had only ever known junk food and take-aways – pizza, burgers, chips, crisps, ice cream, chocolate, biscuits and cake. Without support, how long could he last before he gave in to his cravings? Something else was needed.

But what?

✪✪✪✪✪

Alone at last, spared any more of his parents' vitriolic abuse, George was glad to climb the stairs to bed. From force of habit, he opened the night starvation drawer and allowed his mind to dwell lovingly on the array of chocolate bars, crisps and biscuits. All that fat, sugar and salt.

Suddenly he shivered. It was as if the room had dropped a few degrees. "You can change if you choose." He started, staring around, anxious to find the speaker. "We don't have to be like our parents. We can do anything, be anyone. Just make a start!" It was the other George! It had to be. But the room was empty. And then he was warm again. With one last, lingering look, George firmly closed the night starvation drawer.

The easiest way to break a pot is to drop it. The same is true of a bad habit.

Just drop it.

ELEVENTH COURSE

Knight Makes a Decision

Mr Knight let himself into his private apartment which was situated at the top of the old school. It was a solitary business involving, first, a small door at the side of the building, the resetting of an alarm and the climbing of several flights of stairs. But it was worth it. Centred by a Cubitt tower of the kind much favoured by Queen Victoria at Osborne House, the rooms lay on different levels, each commanding a spectacular view. Knight had all the advantages and disadvantages of "living over the shop." However, thanks to the wily wisdom of a local locksmith, it still managed to be a hiding place that couldn't have been more pupil-proof if situated in the Central Sahara.

He switched on the lights. Golden-shaded lamps cast soft shadows on white walls and walnut furniture. Heavy, green drapes enhanced the décor and shut out the cold. Pouring himself a small Scotch, he pressed a button on the wall and collapsed into the cosy embrace of a large, leather armchair. The haunting strains of Mozart's Clarinet Concerto filled the room and he closed his eyes to experience, more fully, his favourite relaxation therapy. Usually, the combination of Mozart and malt did the trick. But not tonight. He just couldn't get away from the fact that he'd made a complete hash of his meeting with the Guzell parents and that he'd let George down in a spectacular fashion.

It was a full hour before he began to relax. It was nearly another before he went into the kitchen in search of something to eat. Any food he considered reminded him of his encounter with the Guzell family. In the end, he settled for scrambled eggs, large, brown and organic, on slices of multi-grained bread toasted to a light crisp, all washed down with a glass of his favourite Sancerre and followed by fresh fruit.

Later, he found himself going back over the evening's events. He'd been so sure he could swing it: use his clout as Headmaster to influence the parents. It had been a shock to find out that not everybody held him in such high esteem. He paced the floor, rejecting one idea after another. Occasionally, he scribbled down some possibilities, only to cross them out a little later. By midnight, the only thing he knew for certain was that there was no easy answer.

It was dawn when he switched out the light and settled into the troubled sleep that was a forerunner of the equally troubled day ahead.

❂❂❂❂❂

George, for his part, didn't sleep too badly. Like most children, he'd learned to take parental disapproval in his stride. Although he'd seen what had happened with the Headmaster, he hadn't quite accepted that Mr Knight had failed. In George's book, Headmasters don't fail. Somehow, deep down, he believed that Mr Knight would work a miracle.

So, it was no surprise when Mr Knight turned up next morning and asked for him to be excused class. Eagerly, George followed him to his office and, taking the indicated chair, awaited the good news.

"George!" Mr Knight sat down beside him, as he had done on the day when George had cried his eyes out. "George! I am truly sorry!"

George stared. Sorry?

Mr Knight saw his surprise. "You were absolutely right and I was wrong. It was conceited of me to think that I knew your parents better than you do. And I apologise for my misjudgement."

George managed to mutter "It's alright, sir," but his mind shrieked: What do I do now? Mr Knight couldn't meet the agony in George's blue eyes.

The Headmaster took a leaflet from his pocket. "I know it's not much but if you continue to have Mrs D's dinners, watch your calorie intake and increase your exercise, you will make progress. You're bound to. This little book will help you with the calorie count. I'm sorry, George. It's the best I can do."

George managed a dignified exit, headed straight to the cloakroom, where he sat on a row of lockers, and tried to consider his next move. He guessed that Mr Knight was right about watching what he ate and drank and about the exercise. The trouble was that George had hoped for so much more. He wanted day-to-day guidance. He wanted ideas. And he wanted somebody to have faith in him and, when the going got tough, to be there for him. He wished that person could be Sally Larkin, but he knew it was futile. For all her good intentions, she was too young and too inexperienced to provide the back-up he needed. However, without knowing it, he was already making progress. His improved diet had reduced the sugar and fat in his body and this was beginning to affect the quality of his thinking. His mind was clearer, sharper – and quicker – than it had been for years.

Despite his bitter disappointment, despite the fact that Mr Knight had no magic solution to his problems, George was pleased to discover that, for the rest of the day, his mind kept churning out all sorts of new ideas.

TWELFTH COURSE

George Seizes an Opportunity

Days passed. George continued to choose his midday meal from the Dingley/Dulgence Menu. And whilst not exactly enjoying the new taste, which seemed to him to be short of sugar, salt and fat, he did experience a certain self-righteous satisfaction from the effort made. Several times, Sally came to sit next to him. Her presence not only made the food taste better but boosted his standing in the eyes of Sally's long line of admirers. Sometimes, when the meal was over, she would stay and chat, often about the meals George was making for himself at home and sometimes about the progress he was making in class. Sally had been surprised that the boy who'd never taken part in class discussion before, was now speaking up and demonstrating to them all that he had an interesting point of view.

Life at home was no different and, because he couldn't really handle either the shopping or the cooking of a separate meal for himself, it was easier to continue the bad old ways, sharing the customary evening take-away with the rest of the family but eating very much less.

The big difference was in George's attitude.

He had discovered ambition. Now, it was no longer enough merely to fight the flab. Now, his burning desire was to become the slim, handsome George of his alter ego. Powerful medicine! The more he thought about it, the more he knew he could do it. The Head had told him to be a "doer", not a "dreamer". Well, why not?

And then, one evening, he saw and recognised his chance. There, on the front cover of the Radio Times was a picture of Del Dingley. Good looking! Slim! Smiling! Interfering! It was all Dingley's fault. He was the one who had started it. He was the one who'd come to school, mucked about with their food and taken pictures of him, to show everybody in the world what "obese" really looked like. George frowned and angrily flicked the page over. Nobody likes to be picked out for everyone else to mock.

George turned back to the picture and stared at it. Yes, originally, it was Dingley's fault that he was in this mess. Even though he'd come around to the Chef's ideas, he still had many problems. And now, where was Dingley, this stirrer of trouble? On the front cover of the Radio Times. And on TV, making lots of money. But not really telling anyone how to get slim. This man had all the information George needed to make a start and yet he hadn't been seen at school for weeks. An idea was beginning to form… Perhaps this was an opportunity… He was learning that, even when opportunity knocks, a person still has to get off his bottom and open the door. Slowly, methodically, George worked his way through the magazine, cover to cover, all one hundred and forty-six pages, only pausing on the page where the Del Dingley Programme was featured and then going on until he reached the letters page and a telephone number.

"Radio Times. Can I help you?"

"Can I speak to Del Dingley, please?"

"Sorry. No. This is the Editorial Department. If you want to speak to Mr Dingley, you need to contact his programme makers."

George had no idea who they were but a closer inspection of the magazine revealed that the programme was on ITV. He'd often heard other boys speaking about using Google for homework. So, Google it was. George was surprised how easily he found ITV Home – ITV. "Site A-Z Index" looked likely. "Chefs" looked even more promising and there in the list was Del Dingley. He scrolled down and opened up some interesting but not necessarily helpful information about Dingley. Then he saw what he needed. Links. Contact us. The solution to his problem – an address and a telephone number. "Please can I speak to Del Dingley?"

They were nice, very nice, and extremely polite but quite immovable. "Sorry, we don't put through personal calls." The data protection act was mentioned. George didn't know anything about that.

"Well, can you give me a number to ring?" he asked.

"No, sorry, but you can write into the programme and we'll see he gets your letter together with all the others. Mr Dingley receives sack-loads of correspondence every day."

It was many links later that George's persistence was finally rewarded when he discovered that the film production company which made the Del Dingley show for ITV was "DG & C Productions" of Skrifton, Bucks. He phoned, only to be given the same old answer – that Mr Dingley was not available on the phone and that he must write in and mark the letter "Personal." However, the good news was that, if he did this, his letter would be passed to Mr Dingley on the day of its arrival.

George tore a page out of his English exercise book and began to write. But it was no good. He'd never written a letter before and had no idea how or where to begin. A week or two earlier, he'd have given up the struggle at this point, but the new George was made of sterner stuff. Next day, while walking to school, he was still thinking about the problem of the letter.

It was seeing Ella Feakes, Chairperson of the School Council, that gave George his best idea, so far. He followed the bespectacled, bookish Sixth Former down the corridor to the room used by the School Council on occasion and by the sixth form most of the time.

"Ella!" Papers and books cascaded to the floor as George's shout brought the girl to an abrupt halt just as she was about to disappear through a door marked 'Private, Sixth Form.'

A scurry of collection accompanied a contrite George's "Sorry!" as he huffed and puffed to retrieve the last of the papers which had floated off down the corridor.

Ella Feakes focused a pair of owlish bi-focals and stared at the vision of unloveliness before her. "What do you want?"

It was not really an invitation, more a challenge to see if he dared to continue after causing all that disruption. "What's your name?" She groped around for a little black notebook, presumably intending to record his identity. "Don't you know lower school aren't allowed up here?"

George answered "George Guzell" to the first question and nodded agreement to the second.

"Guzell!" She mused and frowned. Failing to completely hide a shudder, she tried to turn it into a shrug and was just about to tell him to get lost when she remembered her duty, as Chairperson of the School Council, to try to help any pupil who approached her with a problem.

"I need to write a letter."

"So, write it!" She put her hand on the door knob and turned away.

"To Del Dingley."

"Del Dingley!" She turned back. This was not what she'd expected to hear.

"Yes, you know, the chef."

"Of course I know, you idiot. He's a celebrity, George. He gets hundreds of letters every day. He probably has a secretary to read them. Save the stamp, why don't you?"

"Please!"

Ella Feakes hesitated. She remembered that George was the boy who kicked up during Del's visit and wasn't it George who only recently caused a scene in the dining hall? "You'd better come in." She opened the door, checked that the room was empty and beckoned George. "Five minutes," she said.

"That's all — and you'd better have something pretty interesting to tell me."

For some moments after George finished speaking, Ella just sat in silence. Normally engaged with complaints about missing sink plugs, shortage of loo paper and closure of the tuck shop, the idea of something more challenging appealed to her. As did the thought that this might be the very thing she'd been looking for — an opportunity for her, perhaps.

"Two names on the letter?" she asked.

"Many as you like." George failed to read her correctly and was just delighted she was going along with it.

"No! No! Two is plenty." Ella had no intention of sharing the opportunity with anyone else and she glared anxiously at her watch to make sure they weren't likely to be interrupted by other inquisitive members of the sixth form. "Yours and mine. And asking — what?"

Two heads bent together, Ella quite forgetting George's scruffy appearance, concerned only with the furtherance of her mission. After George had gone, she engaged in the serious business of composing a well-written request to the TV Chef. Signed first by George and then herself, at the end of afternoon school it was placed in a large envelope marked "Personal," addressed to the Programme Director and taken by her to the Post Office, where she cheerfully paid the extra postage to guarantee delivery the following day.

The Honourable Deborah Smythe-Gibbons, PA to Del Dingley at DG & C Productions, opened the letter on his behalf and cracked out laughing "Darlings! Do listen to this. You know that school you used to start the foody thing...? Well, two pupils have written asking you to go back there to sort some problems. And the scream of it is that one of them is that grotesque creature, Guzell. You know, refused to be interviewed and kicked up one hell of a fuss when he saw himself on telly."

Dingley, getting ready for the tenth take with a bunch of carrots and some herbs, looked decidedly irritated. "For God's sake, Debs! Just deal with it! Like in: no, he's too xxxxxxx busy!"

The PA hesitated. "It says that Guzell has had a change of heart. Needs help to make progress. Thinks you can give it. School dinner programmes aren't going that well. Lot of criticism. Might not

be a bad idea to show that even a barrel of lard like
Guzell can change his tune. Bit of good PR for
you…"

Del executed a neat manoeuvre with diced
carrots and a pan of sizzling mince before reply-
ing, "See what you mean. Get the diary, Debs."

THIRTEENTH COURSE

The Letter

It was a typical December day: dull, dark – fast approaching the shortest day of the year – and cold. Headmaster and teachers had stressed the need for extra clothing or, in the case of some of the older girls, normal clothing. Knight, having returned to his apartment and donned an extra chunky sweater was, even now, standing by the radiator, stamping his feet and warming his hands.

So he was scarcely in cheery, festive mood when he observed a small van driving into the front of the school, reverse parking near the main door and opening rear doors to reveal an array of technical equipment, cameras and crew. "What the...?" Knight flung open the adjoining door. "Janet!" he roared. "What is going on down there?" But his secretary was already on the case, speaking to the front desk and Security.

They received a quick answer with the arrival of a neat, sleek, silver sports car which swung into place beside the van. The occupant, a handsome, dark-haired, fresh-complexioned young man, was instantly besieged by female members of the fourth year who, on their way to the sports field, had caught sight of the TV celeb and stopped to make him welcome.

"Del Dingley!" chorused Knight and Janet.

Knight was furious. "I thought I made it perfectly clear that there were to be no more visits unless agreed in advance by me. I refuse to have the school disrupted. And just think of the problems his last visit created. Get me Security!"

His instructions were crisp and to the point. "Get them out! Now! At once!"

"Sorry, Robert. Too late, I'm afraid. We're already in." Dingley stood in the doorway. "If you still want us to leave when I've finished explaining, we'll go. Without another word of argument. Of course, we will. But when you hear what I have to say, I'm sure you'll wish to reconsider."

As Robert Knight still looked totally unconvinced, Dingley smiled warmly and said,

"Look! Couldn't we just sit down and discuss this?" He sniffed Janet's coffee percolator. "That has to be the best brew I've smelt outside 'The Manx Man', in my home town."

In spite of herself, Janet couldn't help responding to a handsome compliment from a handsome celebrity chef. Immediately, she set a second cup on the tray and, when the two men were seated in Knight's office, she brought it in with a plate of Mrs Dulgence's homemade biscuits.

"You'd better make this good!" Robert Knight waited with no show of forgiveness.

"Well... the long and short of it is that I'm here in answer to a very persuasive letter written by two of your pupils and claimed by them to be an opinion shared by many other students in your school."

"Two pupils here?" The Headmaster combined a frown and a stare.

"Yes. Ella Feakes and George Guzell. Ring any bells?"

"Ella Feakes and George Guzell – together?" Knight's last word squeaked with incredulity. "You're sure about this?"

Dingley searched his pocket, produced a sheet of paper and passed it over to Knight. Well, thought the Headmaster, Guzell never wrote this. Formal school letter heading... Paper obviously nicked from somewhere... He consumed the content quickly.

Dear Mr Dingley,

We should be grateful if you and your camera crew would return to the school and advise further on the correct procedures we should be following to enable us to eat healthily in both school and home. We believe that, for many pupils, the whole business of losing weight is too complex to achieve without the expertise of a specialist.

As you inspired the changes to the content of our school dinners and as problems have ensued, we think it only fair that you should come back to help us with the next step. We should appreciate your kind co-operation in this matter.

We are,
Yours sincerely,

George Guzell and
Ella Feakes, Chairperson of
The School Council.

In spite of himself, Robert Knight chuckled. "I couldn't have put it better myself. They're right, of course: your TV series did leave us with a hell of a lot of problems, some of which are still unresolved. Also, it could be argued that as you started it, you should jolly well finish it. But, in all fairness to you and the team, that may not be quite as simple as our two heroes seem to be suggesting. But, there's a lot you could do, especially with boys like George Guzell who is currently getting his head around the idea that losing weight is not just a vanity but an absolute essential to becoming healthy."

He paused for a moment. "To be honest with you, I really can't contemplate any more disruption in school at this moment. I'm up to my eyes with end-of-term exams, school reports and all the other activities that go to make up Christmas in any school."

"No problem! I'm actually on my way to a shoot, which is why I have the equipment and the crew. We're heading for a run-down restaurant in the Midlands... So, I'm not really looking to take on too much just now. It just didn't seem fair not to give these characters some kind of feedback. After all, you could say I was glad of their help to launch the new dinners idea, so I ought to show willing if they need a follow-up." He leaned forward. "Why don't we speak to them and if there's any mileage in what they're saying, plan a visit at the start of the new term? With your agreement, of course."

Mr Knight was still looking unsure.

"Listen! I know what you're thinking. What's in it for you, for the school? The bottom line is whether you believe that what I'm trying to sell to the kids has any value or not."

Knight thought of his own failed efforts with the Guzell family and of the meagre help he'd been able to offer George.

"Very well," he said, picking up the phone. "Janet, please ask Ella Feakes and George Guzell to come to the office A.S.A.P."

❁❁❁❁❁

The conversation that followed convinced Dingley that there was real potential for him to run a second series. What he needed now, was for

Mr Knight to agree to allow the camera crew on site to record a trailer, for the second series, in the New Year.

It did not take Robert Knight long to realise that he had two options. He could make a fuss and be portrayed as "uncooperative" and "unwilling to help pupils with a problem which was even now giving cause for national concern". Or, he could take the softly, softly approach. No recriminations for Feakes and Guzell. Indeed, compliments for them both – George for his initiative and Ella for the way she'd helped George execute his plan.

❀❀❀❀❀

On their way to the recording of the trailer, George and Ella met in the corridor. "Leave the talking to me," ordered Ella. This was just what she was looking for: the opportunity to show her talents on telly.

"No!" said George.

Ella stopped and stared at him. "What do you mean – 'No!' I thought you hated being on telly, last time?"

"I did. I still do. But it's my idea. My problem. I get to tell Dingley and the viewers and if you've anything to add, you can do it later." George walked ahead, leaving the senior girl looking decidedly miffed. Aware that she'd been put firmly in her place by a boy who was three years her junior and with the IQ of a bag of chips, she also recognised that, currently, George held all the aces. By the time they reached the hall, they found Mr Knight busy keeping out hordes of students who'd taken a 'short cut' to the next lesson via the school hall. Del Dingley was in conference with the producer while the camera crew were making rapid preparations with lighting and cables.

Del, now speaking to camera, was explaining the reason for his being at the school again and then, after introducing George and Ella, he turned back to George.

"So, what is it you want me to do, George? It must be pretty important for you and Ella here, to write on behalf of lots of pupils." George felt himself colouring up with embarrassment and tried to mutter something in reply. "Umm…"

Dingley smiled reassuringly. "Take your time. We'll get it right and then, if you like, we can go again as many times as you wish and then edit out anything we don't want. Incidentally, the last time we came the viewers saw how much you hated being interviewed on telly." He was too kind to add that the boy had scarcely opened his mouth.

George nodded. He pointed to himself. "Look at me! I'm a mess! It wasn't nice being picked out like that. You made me a figure of fun."

Dingley flushed. "I'm sorry," he said. "I hadn't realised. I didn't mean to hurt your feelings... It was insensitive of me... It won't happen again. But why the change of heart?"

George took a deep breath. "Because, although I hated the way you did it, I realise that what you said was true and I have to do something about being obese." He'd said it again, that word. The spirit had said it was a word that only slim people found easy to say. Well, he certainly wasn't anywhere near slim, but perhaps just *wanting to be* counted for something. He saw that Del was waiting for him to go on. "I can't do it alone. I need help."

"Parents?" queried Del.

George shook his head. Mr Knight intervened. "Are you sure you want to say all this on TV, George?"

"Oh, yes!" George was positive. "I don't want to quarrel with Mum and Dad. But I can't let them stop me from getting the help I need. If they won't help, then I've got to find someone else who will."

That should ruffle a few feathers, thought Del Dingley, secretly over the moon. So was his producer. This was the stuff of which memorable interviews are made.

"So what do you need?"

"First of all, we need a cookbook," George replied.

Del pretended his disappointment for the camera. "There are hundreds out there. I'd think you'd be spoilt for choice. Any good bookshop can help you."

Mr Knight chimed in: "Cookbooks? The school library's full of them."

"Not like this, there aren't," said George, who was the only one not acting a part.

"Not like what, George?" asked Del.

"You know, like Mrs Dulgence has, but one we can use at home." He looked across at Ella. "I told you to speak up if there was something else to say. Tell him what I mean."

Ella was delighted to take the floor. This was the moment she'd been waiting for. "What George wants," she explained, "is a cookbook that will include all the good-for-you menus you have suggested for the school canteen but so clearly written that anybody, even a first former, could understand and cook from it. If we're all going to lose weight, just having good-for-you food at school is never going to be enough."

"You mean – a cookbook for kids?" Del spoke slowly as if his mind whizzed with a new idea – but it was really one he had prepared earlier.

George nodded. "Yes, something easy."

Del Dingley also nodded. He was well pleased with the way the interview was going. Wait till his publisher heard about it. "Oh, I think we can manage that for you, George. Great idea! Anything else?"

"Well…" Suddenly, the fat boy looked so weary. For a lad who had never been in the limelight, except in the worst possible way, this was a powerful mixture. "There's just so much more." He looked across at Ella. "She can explain it better then me."

Something in George's face touched the heart of the normally self-interested older girl. Perhaps it was his sheer despair. She was unusually gentle as she took up the story. "George thinks that we ought to have a school project that covers everything connected to diet, healthy eating, exercise and, losing weight."

Mr Knight, listening attentively, couldn't help interrupting. The camera swung in his direction. "You mean stop all formal lessons and try to link all subjects to the one main topic?" His teacher's mind leapt quickly to interesting side issues. "Place of food in history, recent developments, value of vitamins, calories, countries which produce good-for-you or bad-for-you food…" The Producer signalled time. It was still George's show. "Sorry," Mr Knight laughed. "I was getting quite carried away." He grimaced. "Of course, we'll have to talk to everybody – staff, pupils and parents – about such a massive disruption of the timetable."

The Producer indicated for Ella and George to continue but again it was Ella who spoke. "George and I," Ella dazzled him with a smile of inclusion, "discovered that in two years' time, one fifth of the nation's children – that's almost a million – will be obese unless we do something about it." Democratically, she added: "Perhaps, we should call a meeting of the School Council and then George can tell everyone about it."

"I'm not a member of the Council," George put in, feeling very pleased that Ella should ever have thought he was.

"You are now," Ella announced. "I'm making a unilateral decision to co-opt you onto the Council, as it's for the good of the whole school." The recording ended.

George Guzell grew! He'd never known before what it felt like to really "stand tall". And he had to admit it felt great!

FOURTEENTH COURSE

Emergency Meeting of the School Council

A group of interested spectators hung round the School Council notice board next day. The small fry knew something was afoot but could only make outlandish guesses at what; Middle School had even less idea but pretended a lot more, while Upper School stood about, talking in hushed voices of the seriousness of the matter which had precipitated this action.

Ella Feakes had called an Emergency Meeting of the School Council, something unheard of in the recent history of Upper School and quite surprising because it was only a week since the usual monthly meeting at which there had been no "outstanding business" or any suggestion of forthcoming problems.

With no clues, and no other way to find out, every bench, chair, window seat and even every step was taken. It was a long time since the School Council had attracted such a crowd.

As usual, the meeting was opened by Chairperson Feakes who, after going through all the correct committee procedures from Minutes of previous meeting to non-existent apologies for absence, had introduced a "guest speaker" whom, she said, wished to appraise the school of certain new issues which vitally concerned them all.

A hushed silence ensued, shattered by a sudden excited hubbub when the Council realised that the mysterious "guest speaker" was none other than that mountainous member of the Third Year, George Guzell.

Had the unbelievably smart teenager finally taken leave of her senses?

Their misgivings were confirmed when Ella announced that she'd taken it upon herself to co-opt George onto the Council proper. Forestalling two members of the Sixth Form whose academic aspirations nearly matched her own, she told them "This decision was not taken lightly, but in the belief that the action was justified, being in the best interest of the school." Murmurings of agreement and head-noddings allowed some, who hadn't so far understood any of the proceedings, to pretend that they were all on the same wavelength.

Everybody waited for George, and the one or two who started the usual Georgy Porgy routine were quickly shut up by the rest – if only because they thought that George's attempt to make a speech would probably be infinitely more amusing.

What a pathetic object! thought Ella, giving George a short, sharp shove in the back to remind him that he was required to do something – like speaking!

"Come on, George. You can't let me down now!" Ella whispered, exerting a firm hold on his arm. George took up a position centre front and then looked at his audience. For a long moment he just stared. To his amazement, he realised the noise was subsiding. His confidence boosted, he waited until he had complete silence. "I'm fat!" he announced. Roars of laughter. "You're fat, too!" He pointed at the front row. Not quite so many people laughed this time and the victim looked away. "And so are you, and you, and you, and you!" Nobody was laughing now. People were trying not to catch his eye.

"Actually," said George in a matter-of-fact tone, "I'm more than fat. I'm obese!"

Chairs scraped. Feet shuffled. Some over-large members of the Council tightened stomach and buttock muscles. The particularly over-large adopted an ostrich policy and dug themselves lower into chairs and benches, hoping that if they couldn't see George, then he couldn't see them.

"Obese," said George, "is dangerous. Really dangerous! All of us who are obese," he smiled, "I won't pick you out. You know who you are. You could die from all sorts of illnesses if you don't do something about it. I used to be annoyed when people said I was obese. It's annoying when people disagree with you, especially when they're right. And they were right."

The school was listening in a way it hadn't listened to Dingley, Knight, Champion or all the well-meaning messages on TV. They could see the deep misery inside George and understood that he was genuinely trying to save them from the same fate. George sensed that, somehow, the atmosphere in the meeting had improved. For once, they were on his side. "Some of you," he said, "are eating the new food." Grumblings from the back. "I know – I felt just the same a little while ago." If only he could tell them about the spirits, but Ella (in whom he had confided) had been adamant that if he wanted any credibility with this lot, he had to forget them.

"No ghosts, George," she hissed.

George nodded and took up his story again. "Today, I know I was wrong. If we're going to beat this thing, this huge problem," he patted his stomach and waited for the laughter to die down before continuing: "we've got to look at everything we eat and drink. We've got to listen to people who know much more about food than we do, and we've got to stop being stupid about it and take notice." He was amazed that he still had their attention. "Yesterday," George told them, "Ella and I met Del Dingley." They were impressed and showed it. George felt himself growing again. His shoulders straightened.

Sally Larkin noticed too; noticed what a nice smile George had and the proud way he'd said "Ella and I." Talking to Del Dingley! The two of them together! No way! Not if she had anything to do with it.

"We told him," George continued, gaining confidence (he'd noticed Sally smiling at him), "We told him that we needed help in two ways. First, we asked him to write a special cookbook – something we can all understand and use easily in the kitchen at home because it will be specially written for people who have never cooked." Nods of approval. "And then, we asked Mr Knight if we can have time, school time, to turn this whole thing into a big school project, and have Del to help us."

Cheers all round. The swots loved the idea – more time spent with books and on computers. The skivers loved the idea too – they saw an opportunity to sit back and do nothing.

"You mean, a no-ordinary-lesson-type-project?" enquired the boy George had first pointed out as fat. George nodded. Suddenly, he felt unspeakably weary. Excitement and being at the centre of the action were so new that the very joy of it all was sapping his energy.

Ella interpreted the situation and smoothly took over. "Shall I fill in some of the detail, George?"

She consulted a paper. "The project will start in the New Year and all subjects will be linked to good health, diet, food values, history of food, growing of food, exercise, etc. We think that, in one way or another, every subject should be able to make a contribution."

"How long?" somebody shouted. The Council held its collective breath.

Ella gave them her most sincere, non-conspiratorial look. "It could be as much as a month or as little as a week, depending on how seriously we all take the project. Realistically, I reckon three weeks."

Nice one, thought the Headmaster from his vantage point in the upper gallery where, shielded by the organ, he could listen without being seen. Miss Feakes should go far. Certainly as far as the House of Commons. But it was George who had really interested him, first with Dingley and now here in front of the School Council. Was it really possible, he wondered, that less fat, less sugar and less salt could change a boy so dramatically and in so little time? It was too early to see any noticeable weight loss but something had sharpened George's mind. Maybe all that talk on TV about diet and additives was right. Maybe he really would be justified in giving the project his full backing.

Down below, Ella was drawing the meeting to a close, reminding everyone that the Head would be sending letters to parents, (so these were definitely not ones to intercept) and that Del Dingley would be with them in the second week of term.

"You did well, George," complimented Ella, shaking hands. She was surprised to find that she actually meant it. Something about George's performance had both moved and amazed her. George felt pleased with himself, too. To his surprise, he'd really enjoyed making a speech to a large audience and bending them to his will, or trying to. He felt a new power, as if the world was at his feet.

❂❂❂❂❂

In the few weeks that followed to the end of term, being fat and enjoying Christmas went together perfectly. Most people (except George) felt it was not the season to count calories. Not for the first time, Mr Knight blessed the foresight of his ancestor Worthington Knight who'd left a sum of money specifically for the provision of food and drink to celebrate the festivities. Wisely invested over the years, the legacy had grown until, even at today's prices, its interest was more than enough to pay for a good meal for the whole school. Against a backdrop of Christmas celebrations, plans for the school's new health project were perfected and those concerned with balancing the school's books assessed the extra funding such a venture would require.

Form parties and the traditional pantomime preceded the school's carol concert when the big band led the pupils and local residents in a rousing singsong, this year conducted, appropriately enough, amidst a flurry of snowflakes. Day by day, the excitement grew, reaching a magnificent climax on the last full day of term when staff and pupils shared Christmas Dinner. All morning, the school warmed to the tantalising aroma of seventy succulent, slow-roasting turkeys accompanied by strings of sizzling sausages and trays of crispy, crunchy, golden roast potatoes.

Dorothy Dulgence surpassed herself, more than deserving the "thank you" flowers presented by the school's youngest pupil.

But turkey was only the start. There was still the moment they'd all been waiting for – the dimming of lights, the loud screams from the girls, and the entry of the school choir carrying red, ceremonial-size candles. And there, ahead of the inevitable Father Christmas, was Gruff himself, carrying the largest Christmas pudding they were ever likely to see.

The command to "Be upstanding!" heralded the lighting of the vodka and brandy-soaked pudding into a flambéed circle of electric-blue flames, which was followed, almost at once, by the release of hundreds of red and green balloons, streamers and other nonsensical toys just to make sure that the school's moment of madness continued long into the afternoon.

Only George remained somewhat aloof from the proceedings. For the first time in his life, he was enjoying school and the many challenges it offered. To him, Christmas meant more food, more family and more friction. For the Guzell family had, by then, discovered that George had broadcast to the entire viewing world the fact that they refused to help him in his fight to beat the flab.

What George most wanted for Christmas was – the day after.

FIFTEENTH COURSE

The Project

Winter solstice over. New Year resolutions made and broken... Any goodwill long gone, blown away by short, dark days and long, cold nights... The Health Project was a godsend.

The first to arrive were the nurses from the local health centre, bearing scales and blood pressure monitors. The initial task was to make sure that everyone was fit to take part and to furnish all the pupils with their own vital statistics so that progress could be measured.

At the end of the previous term, letters home had explained the plans to parents, urging them to seek their GP's advice if they had any reservations about their child's involvement in the school's get-fit scheme. Target dates, by which it was hoped everybody would have the backing of parents and nurse or doctor, were issued.

Banners floated from the Cubitt tower and flag-pole encouraging the school and local community to "Eat lean, Eat fresh, Eat green." Food-pyramids decorated every dining table showing the differing levels of good-for-you-dishes with the broad base urging pasta, cereal, fruit and vegetables and narrowing upwards through yoghurt and cheeses, meat and poultry to the apex with its not so good-for-you fats and sweets.

Science and Maths looked at the food industry's use of trans fats, studied cholesterol levels, defined saturated and unsaturated fats and worked out each pupil's BMI – Body Mass Index – a formula to establish whether one is underweight, normal, overweight or obese. Subjects that teachers had struggled to "sell" months ago were now much in demand. Some members of staff who normally enjoyed a certain anonymity found themselves, almost overnight, bewildered by their rise to popularity and overwhelmed by the number of questions fired at them on corridors, in the dining hall and, even, in the street. Their knowledge was in demand. Hardly surprising! Pupils and teachers were glimpsing their reflections in the long, shatter-proof mirrors now strategically placed in corridors and cloakrooms – and noticing bulges and folds of flesh they did not know they had. PE staff drew up a variety of exercise programmes, stressing the need for moderation in all things.

The whole school joined together to create calorie counting charts, designed and printed by Art and Print Departments and based upon research by the Science Department. These were hung behind every door and placed in every desk and locker. They covered various sporting activities from football (400 calories), through basketball (500) to – best of all – running (550). These charts also included everyday activities like sitting and reading (15), getting dressed (50), ironing (80), cooking (95), washing the dishes (95), and carpentry (160). If you did it, the chart covered it. Just running up and down the stairs was a fantastic calorie burner (250). School chat took a new turn. "What grade did she give you?" was replaced with "How many calories did you burn?" Delighted parents described how children who had never lifted a finger around the house were actually asking to help to vacuum (110) or paint walls (170). But the main message was always the same: the best exercise of all is to exercise restraint at the dinner table.

Mental arithmetic improved as if by magic and the Biology teacher, who'd previously lost sleep trying to make vitamins and minerals interesting, was astonished to find that, when it came to a good, wholesome diet, her pupils absorbed facts and figures as if they were all aspiring scientists. Any pupil could tell you that Vitamin B2 (Riboflavin) was to be found in dairy produce, leafy vegetables, liver, kidneys and yeast.

The school garden was revived and transformed. It seemed like everybody wanted to help there. Although hardly the right time for planting, there was no shortage of labourers willing to ply spade, fork and hoe, satisfied that they were winning on two counts: calorie burning and preparing the land.

Every subject played a part. History classes looked at population figures and considered why the nation had not only grown in number but also in height and width of individuals. They examined minutely the pre-1939 diet compared with that brought in by the government during WW2. As George's great grandfather had suggested, the nation as a whole was infinitely healthier then than now, despite wartime rationing. Geographers concentrated on food resources, gluts and famines and why, despite the combined efforts of the World

Health Organisation and other well-meaning bodies, no one seemed to have found a lasting solution. It was noticeable during this period that, after Geography lessons, many pupils ate less and few wasted their food. George and many others felt ashamed of their enormously overweight bodies in the light of the starvation of the under-developed parts of the world. George couldn't forget what the second spirit had shown him – the woman who walked miles for water and the child who just lay there by the roadside, waiting to die.

As promised, Del Dingley returned. Previously regarded with a certain scepticism, he was now greeted like a long-lost friend. This was the man who'd started it all and whose ideas had now led the school to one of its favourite creations – the Project.

His first stopping place was the school's kitchen where Mrs Dulgence was eager to share her trials and tribulations, but also her successes and her belief that, slowly but surely, the tide was turning in her favour. Within minutes, Del had his sleeves rolled up and was demonstrating a new pudding which would gladden the hearts of all pudding-lovers without adding inches to their middles.

His second place was Robert Knight's office, where the two men discussed "ways and means". Money was still a problem. The tuck shop had been a money-making enterprise. Its change to healthy snacks had been expensive and unpopular, while healthy alternatives in the dining hall cost more. Good-quality food, even basic good-quality food, was dearer than junk food, something some parents still didn't want to know about. Or perhaps they genuinely believed that the cheaper junk food was really doing no harm? "I'll talk to them again," he promised. "Our best hope is that the kids will do our talking for us. They're the ones who can really convince their parents that spending a bit more is a long-term good investment." But not all was doom and gloom. Some of the parents, who had been aggressively hostile to his ideas because they saw him as an interfering busybody were now coming into school to buy calorie charts for themselves and to look for diet sheets.

George had become Dingley's protégé – the teenage boy likely to make the most progress – partly because he was able to convince his peers that if he could do it, so could they; partly because he could make the most spectacular weight loss because he had more of it to lose. That the Guzell family were not on board added to George's apparent success. He was doing it alone, for all the right reasons, and he set an excellent example for all those teenagers wanting to be slim, despite their parents' lack of support. There was a surprisingly high number of such parents. Indeed, in another area, parents had actually handed take-away meals through the school railings rather than let their offspring acquaint themselves with food which was wholesome and nutritious.

George was interviewed on TV again. This time, Del was careful to treat the teenager with some respect, recognising that his earlier interview had been insensitive. They talked about Christmas and George explained how difficult it had been to make progress in a house where no one else wanted to know about eating healthy food. They talked about the new cookbook, with George being given the chance to suggest things he'd like to see included. Programme ratings implied that it was largely due to George that so many teenagers were now watching. He even received fan mail and Ella was delighted to help with the replies. She too, was making headway with the producer who, though he thought Ella was "a bit of a pain," admitted she was just the sort to forge her way ahead on the administrative side of the media.

In each programme, Del and George used a make-shift kitchen with minimum equipment and

Del showed George how to prepare a simple meal quickly and safely. To Del, the Project, the cookbook, the buying of convenience food all spelled out one question for parents: "When did you last cook a proper meal in your kitchen?" This was what he always asked the viewers when the end credits rolled.

Within a month, including Christmas, George's personal chart showed that he'd lost some weight; not a lot, but enough to be encouraging. His body began to take a less random shape. His face firmed up and lost its resemblance to a balloon. He discovered he could walk without making frequent stops to get his breath. On a good day, there was even an attempt at a spring in his step: a sort of tentative, virtual spring.

"His clothes are beginning to hang on him," observed Del to his producer, as he and George made their way to the mock kitchen. That night, Del rang the programme's sponsor. Within days a new school uniform had appeared and the viewing public heard that George had actually gone down a size.

"I can't pay for that," George frowned. "I haven't got the money and my parents definitely won't help."

"Call it "a present from a well-wisher". Can't have your pants falling down in the middle of a shoot."

So why, in the midst of all this progress, did George feel distinctly depressed? He was losing weight. He was making quite a name for himself on TV. One or two people had actually stopped him in the street to ask for his autograph. With a bit of luck, lots of encouragement and some hard work on his part, it really looked as if he would influence the eating habits of many people for the better.

Only one thing spoiled what should have been the happiest of times: the refusal of his parents to take any sort of interest in the new George. He told himself that he didn't care. If they didn't want to be involved, well, that was their problem – not his. The truth was not so simple. All children hope for parental approval and teenage George was no exception. He wanted them to share in his progress and to be proud of his success.

Apart from anything else, deep down, he was afraid that, when all the TV lights were dimmed and the school project was over, he might not be able to carry on without their help.

SIXTEENTH COURSE

The Penny Drops

George was in the school library, looking in the local paper for any pictures there might be of himself and Del, when a quite different item on an inside page caught his attention. At first, he read it without realising its significance. It was a report about the great torrent of counterfeit films which had flooded Britain in the form of cheap DVDs. The article said that thousands of blank DVDs were smuggled into the country, mainly from Malaysia. These were sold on to local pirates who used their own DVD recorders to make copies from illegally obtained "preview films" of popular movies which they then sold for considerably less than the legitimate price. The article explained that despite their inferior quality, there had been massive sales of such pirate DVDs in the local area and the police believed that the counterfeits were being recorded locally.

George read it again. Suddenly, the penny dropped. Suddenly, Mr Knight's visit to the house filled his mind. He had a vivid recollection of his father's concern to move all those piles of DVDs away from Gruff's chair, a concern which had caused Ivor to get up from his own chair, something he only ever did reluctantly at moments of dire necessity. He tried to remember the name of the film he had seen on the DVD that had dropped at Mr Knight's feet. Something about the... *Web Wonderman* – That was it!

For five minutes he just sat there, thinking. He kept adding two and two and, amazingly, constantly making four.

"Hello, George! I'm pleased to see that you're interested in local affairs." It was a smiling Mr Knight standing over him. George had been so absorbed in the newspaper, he'd not noticed the Headmaster coming into the library. Startled by the suddenness of the encounter, he hastily turned the page, muttered something, made his excuses and left.

Knight was well aware of George's discomfort, probably connected with whatever he'd been reading. What could possibly have gripped the teenager's attention in a way which none of the school's lessons ever had? Although his view of the paper had been upside down, he'd noticed the page as it carried a half-page advert for a local store. Knight sat down at the table, picked up the paper and located the exact page. George's attention had been focused on something at the bottom of the page. There was only one item down there: "Pirate DVDs Flood Area".

After reading the article, Knight surmised that George had probably purchased some of these pirated DVDs and feeling guilty, didn't want his Headmaster to know.

✪✪✪✪✪

Later that evening, George's worst suspicions were confirmed by an item on TV. The presenter was enthusing over the forthcoming comedy *Web Wonderman,* which would have its premiere in a West End cinema next week, prior to going on general release. But George had already seen the same film on DVD, apparently one of a box full in his own home during Mr Knight's visit.

George had very little sleep that night. His thoughts were gloomy. If word got out that his parents were pirating DVDs, it would be "good-bye" to filming with Del Dingley. Worse! If his parents were arrested, what would happen to Hatty and himself? Would they be put into care? He fretted about who best to ask for advice. His Gran? But she might tell his dad. Ella? But would Ella know what to do in this instance? Del Dingley? Would a celebrity chef get involved with something illegal? Hardly! That left only one person.

George was outside Mr Knight's door at ten to nine.

The Headmaster was surprised. He'd seen little of George in recent weeks except as an on-looker when Dingley was filming. "Well, George, please take a seat… And how may I help?"

George sank into one of the Head's chairs, noticing that his ample buttocks now slid easily into place. Mr Knight waited. George cleared his throat. "Sir, you know how, sometimes, in a film, a man goes into a church and talks to a priest behind a kind of screen and says: 'I'm going to tell you something that you mustn't tell anyone else.'?"

"I think we're talking about the secrets of the confessional, George," interrupted Knight, hoping this conversation wasn't going to be as difficult as the one they'd had previously, concerning the spirits.

George beamed. "That's right, sir."

"The thing is, George, in such films, the confessions usually concern something very serious, like a murder. I hope you're not going to tell me that you've killed anyone." He looked at George, enquiringly.

"Oh no, sir. It's not a murder. But it is something very serious – and against the... And it wasn't me who did... I'm confessing for someone else."

"Ah! I see! Confessing for someone else! And do I understand this someone else wishes to remain anonymous?"

"Oh, yes, sir. In fact, they don't even know that I'm doing this for them. But don't you worry, sir – they would never murder anyone."

"They–?" Knight thought quickly. "Supposing we keep this conversation to a hypothetical case, George. You know: we both pretend that you're making up a story, without names being mentioned. Lets us both off the hook if you see what I mean." He saw that George did not see, so explained further. "You can ask anything you like and I can answer how I like, but we are neither of us committing ourselves because what we say is not linked to any real person. It is just talk in general... Theoretical... Unrelated... Hypothetical... In this way, we can explore all sorts of answers quite freely and confidentially."

George nodded. "Hypothetical! Right!" Mr Knight waited for him to begin. "So, what would you do if you discovered," George paused, "hypothetically, of course, that somebody close to you was doing something illegal?"

"Well, hypothetically, of course, one should have to ask oneself two questions. Is the crime so bad that it is one's duty to tell the police? Or, is it possible that one could bring these activities to an end simply by talking to those concerned and letting them know that one knows what they're up to?"

"But supposing you thought that, because you were young, they might not take any notice?"

"Ah! I see! Yes… Maybe you could make them take notice by warning them that if they continued to break the law, you'd tell the police. Alternatively, you might be able to force them to do something else, something very good – to make up for their previous crimes."

"Isn't that blackmail, sir?" George enquired.

The Head seemed surprised. "You have me there, George! You may be right. Although blackmail is usually carried out for selfish reasons, like making easy money, not to do good. The question is whether the end justifies the means." He looked at his watch. "Sorry! Got to fly. Fifth Year Assembly in thirty seconds."

That afternoon, George feigned a headache and left school early. Very quietly, he let himself in by the back door. He walked straight into the sitting room where he found a flustered Nora and Ivor packing DVDs into boxes.

"What do you want?" His mother was less than welcoming. "I thought you were supposed to be poncing about with Mr Smart-arse Dingley."

George sat on the edge of the settee. "Sorry to bother you, Mum, but there are a few things we have to talk about…"

❂❂❂❂❂

The year following George's chat with his mother brought many changes. It started to improve even in the first months of the New Year. The worst of the winter was over. Spring was not quite here but there was a gentleness in the air not unnoticed by George who, as usual these days, walked home in the company of several boys from his class.

In a few short weeks, life had turned a corner. Already more than a stone lighter, George was no longer alone. He had many friends. He had good food – not fast, but fresh. With Del Dingley's help, he was beginning to appreciate new tastes and textures and to reap the physical rewards.

He pushed open the garden gate, wondering what meal his mother had prepared, for she now cooked for the entire family and take-aways were a thing of the past. George smiled at the garden plants as he walked along the path. The weeds had gone. The scrubby lawn had gone, too. Instead, there was deep, dark soil, newly turned and ready for planting.

His mother was in the kitchen. The stove was full of pans. The table was set. His father was in his customary chair and breathing deeply. He was wearing his new track suit, recently purchased following an extended search to find one big enough. "Been running again, Dad?"

Ivor groaned, which George interpreted as a "Yes".

"Do you want to go to the football tonight?" George's ears nearly fell off. He couldn't remember the last time he and his dad had been anywhere together.

"Great, Dad! Great!" Female voices off roared that the meal was ready. A bowl of savoury mince and another of pasta stood waiting.

"Well?" his mother snapped. She'd lost none of her bite but George couldn't help noticing that she looked different somehow. "Well?" The menace was still there.

"Mmm… smells good." George consulted his little book. Pasta was great. Right at the base of the school's food pyramid (89 calories). And the mince?

"Best beef," snapped Nora. "Fat drained off. Garlic, herbs and lots of onions." She offered a bowl of freshly grated Parmesan. "You can have a bit of this. It's a hard cheese," she told him. "You don't need much. But it adds a lot of flavour."

For a moment, he wondered if he were back in the dream but the heat of the food and the presence of Mum, Dad and Princess told him differently. He lifted spoon and fork. "Fantastic!" Fresh fruit followed, all washed down with sparkling water.

While they ate, they talked – another recent innovation. Nowadays, the family enquired about his day or told him about theirs or, even, asked his opinion. Recently, he found himself looking at them all in a new light. They really weren't so bad. The memory of the last spirit was still very much in his mind. The thought that they might be going to an early grave had preyed on him ever since that night.

He so wanted them to be happy and live long enough to be a part of his future life.

Today, there was something different about his parents, something strange. And then, he knew! "Are you…?" His voice was thick with emotion. He was terrified to finish the question in case he'd got it wrong. "Are you… slimming?" He whispered the words, especially the last one.

"Give him a medal!" His father groaned a delighted groan. George smiled. Give him a medal… He'd heard that phrase before. Mort would have been pleased.

"We thought you'd never notice." Nora sounded almost coy. Their grins stretched from ear to ear. "Dad's lost three pounds and I've lost a couple. Princess has only just got going. But from now on we're in it with you, son. All the way." George beamed with pleasure for the rest of the day and right through the football match, even though the homeside lost.

It was, indeed, the icing on the carrot cake. Up to that point, George had been doing quite well; but now, with the entire family fighting the flab, his progress was spectacular. There were no more spirits of the night. No more agonising interviews with the Headmaster although, from time to time, he heard from Mr Champion that Gruff was well pleased with his improvement.

As time passed and the grotesque mounds of fat disappeared, a strikingly handsome young man began to take shape. Everyone noticed the change, especially the girls. Sally Larkin seemed to pop up round every corner. If he went to the gym, she was – by chance – waiting outside when he'd finished. When he walked home from school she was there, trying to give the impression that, quite by chance, she'd arrived at that same spot when he did. Whenever he and Ella were off in a huddle with Del Dingley, there was always a figure lurking somewhere in the background – keeping tabs.

And Del Dingley was quick to capitalise on George's progress by televising the teenager as many times as he could. After all, Dingley had a vested interest. George's transformation from chair-breaker to heart-breaker, when seen on TV, was as useful as a million-pound advertising campaign. It occurred to Dingley that what the Great British viewing public needed more than anything else was a programme about the Del Dingley Diet for Schools, featuring George and of course, Dingley's best-selling *Cookbook for Kids*. All it would need was some new, specially shot material and existing footage linked together by his own cheery on-screen presentation.

SEVENTEENTH COURSE

Prize-Giving Day

As the months passed, George grew tall and slim. He learned that dieting didn't mean going without, but choosing wisely. It meant exercising more: cricket in summer, football in winter. It meant eating to live, not living to eat. As his body changed, so did his mind. He moved up the class and when Prize-Giving Day came round, he proudly escorted his fitter, younger-looking parents to their seats at the front of the hall.

That year, the celebrity invited to make the speech was an obvious choice. The whole school cheered as Del Dingley, accompanied by the Head, took his place on the platform. For a few minutes, no one attempted to speak against the clapping of hands and stamping of feet. When the applause died down, the Headmaster said: "Please remain standing for a moment, everyone."

Del Dingley advanced to the edge of the platform and said: "Excuse me, but I want to take a closer look at you." He then peered down at the rows of self-consciously smiling faces for several seconds as though inspecting them all. Suddenly, he smiled and said: "Thank you very much – I must say that you are a much healthier-looking lot than when we first met. Well done! That just shows what a difference a proper diet makes. Now give yourself a round of applause."

Then he presented the prizes. As the last one was placed in his hands, he stepped up to the microphone. "The final prize," he said, "is one that is dear to the heart of everybody in this room – it is particularly dear to your Headmaster, and to me... It's about dedication, discipline, and diet. It's about courage, commitment and calories. It's about energy, enthusiasm and exercise. It's about a boy who dreamed these things and set about turning them into a reality. Although many of you deserve prizes, there can be only one winner and you all know who it is. The Del Dingley Prize for the Student Who Has Made the Greatest Physical Improvement goes to... George Guzell!"

When the applause finally died down, George stepped forward. The school waited. Cameras flashed. Reporters poised with mini-recorders were at the ready. They were all used to George having something to say to them: something they'd want to hear. There was so much he wanted to say and so much of it nobody would have believed.

"I want to thank my family for helping make this happen," he began. The new slim-line Nora, Ivor and Hatty all straightened their shoulders and beamed. Somewhere, George hoped that Great Grandpa Mort was listening and that he and the other spirits would realise that he meant them, too.

"And I promise... I won't let you down," he said. "I won't let you down." He'd already learned from experience that no speech is entirely bad if it is short enough.

In the long term, George was better than his word. He did all that he'd promised and more. He continued to lose weight and backed up that loss by regular exercise, so that muscles that had been flabby and weak became tough and strong.

To his parents and sister, none of whom died young, he was a source of pride and inspiration. Eventually, he and Sally Larkin became an item. But things had changed and these days Sally felt that she had to do all the running just to stay with him. Now, George had a following – other girls who fancied the cool young teen on their TV screens. And then there was the ever-present Ella who was still involved in any discussions regarding the school's involvement in the TV programme.

And the media continued to follow the story. The fat boy, who'd come from nowhere into their lives, was still worth watching. From time to time he was interviewed on TV or asked to write an article about slimming for a magazine or newspaper. To have evolved from "Lard Mountain" to "Action Hunk" and to have done so while the process was being recorded on TV and watched by millions, had made George into Britain's most celebrated slimmer at a time in history when it is possible to achieve celebrity for far less – "celebrity" being the modern term for "hero".

On the day he finally left university clutching a very respectable degree, a sealed envelope awaited his return. It was from his old mentor, Del Dingley, inviting him to join the creative team at DG & C Productions for a new TV series.

EIGHTEENTH COURSE

Aftermath

Two years later, Robert Worthington Knight and his Deputy Jack Champion were celebrating the end of term with a very good bottle of claret in the Head's private apartment. They switched on the TV to catch the first in a new series: *George Guzell's Eat Yourself Slim*. The programme ended with a big close-up of a lean, handsome George smiling his most captivating smile as his catchy, specially-composed signature tune blared forth.

Knight switched off the set and topped up the glasses for a toast to George's success. "Well, all those years ago, when he was having Dickensian nightmares, who would have thought it?" said Knight.

"You did, Headmaster!" laughed Jack.

"Oh, no… I never dreamt he'd be so successful.

I just wanted him to lose the flab and do his best..."

"Well, he has certainly done both... But are you telling me that it was George who sorted out his parents? How on earth did he do that?"

Knight smiled and sipped his wine reflectively. He'd never told anyone about his 'hypothetical' conversation with George.

"Yes, it was George. As to how he did it – who can say? Perhaps he appealed to their better natures... Or perhaps he found an argument persuasive enough to win over his parents... Anyway, good luck to him!"

Jack Champion raised his glass. "Good luck to George!" he toasted.

Privately, Knight breathed a sigh of relief. The fewer people who knew the real truth, the better. And the real truth, as far as Knight understood it, was that George had reformed his eating habits because he'd seen the light, while his parents had reformed theirs because they'd felt the heat.

Epilogue

Another Christmas Eve, a decade later, in a restored manor house somewhere on the outskirts of the picturesque village of Little Brassington, lights twinkled on the large Norwegian Spruce, holly and mistletoe hung in be-ribboned garlands and a sweet-smelling log fire illuminated leather-bound books and old paintings. Candlelight shone on the Venetian glass punchbowl, surrounded by straw baskets of mince pies all awaiting the arrival of the village carol singers at dusk.

George glanced at the Rolex on his wrist and sank back into the depths of the luxurious leather sofa. Half an hour to himself! Luxury! Contrary to what most people believe, being a celebrity does not guarantee much of your own space. Not that George was complaining – far from it. Even so, he was glad that today, of all days, he had time for reflection: an opportunity to remind himself just how lucky he had been.

Many people would have said that luck didn't come into it and that George was the perfect example of someone who'd made his own luck through willpower and hard work. But George, despite his phenomenal success, was still a modest man who firmly believed that fate had been remarkably kind to him.

Eyes half shut, he spanned the past. How many years ago had he chosen to be like his alter ego? How long since he'd flung open the windows of this very house to shout, like Scrooge: "I did it! I did it! I did it!"

And he had, too: gradually losing another five stone, catching up on his education, and all the while being the focus of public attention as people followed and aped his every move.

A woman, carrying a sleeping child, came into the room and sat down beside him. He stretched out an arm and drew them close. "I was just thinking…" he began, softly.

She smiled. It was a tender, loving smile. "I know George. I know exactly what you were thinking. I always do a bit of thinking myself on Christmas Eve." They were both quiet now, each concerned with their own memories.

❂❂❂❂❂

While George's size had been diminishing and his fame growing, Ella Feakes had been getting on with her own life more or less anonymously. Leaving Oxford, with a completely predictable First Class Honours degree, she went straight into a job as a college lecturer. But after five years she had had enough of academia, so she tendered her notice and went off in search of her own dream – a job in the media.

It had seemed only natural to apply to George's company and equally natural that he should conduct the interview. After all, hadn't they known each other for years? "Ella! What a pleasure!" His voice, smooth as clotted cream, had very nearly added, "And what a surprise!" Momentarily dazzled by emerald green eyes no longer shielded by bi-focals, he felt unnerved. Ella felt reassured by his gaze but – she drew breath sharply – it was as if he saw everything from her elegant La Perla knickers to the tiny birthmark on her left breast. She bore his scrutiny bravely. If there was one thing Oxford had taught her, apart from the obvious, it was better to be looked over than overlooked. Today, Fenella Feakes knew she was sexy as well as savvy.

"George!" She sat down, gracefully, crossing her long legs, aware that his eyes appraised the short skirt of her classic, black Valentino suit and glad that she was wearing her four-inch heeled Jimmy Choos. "It's good to see you." She swept the shoulder length bob of rich brunette hair from her face and slowly moistened the lips of her Chanel Absolute Rouge.

George Guzell was mesmerised. The white, silk slip peeping through the well-fitting jacket; the finely crafted, gold choker highlighting the column of slender neck; the matching red Chanel bag and gloves; and the consummate ease of the wearer all added to the picture of perfection that was the wonderfully elegant Fenella (definitely not Ella) Feakes.

While he took stock, all the while seemingly rifling through a pile of papers in search of her CV, she had the time to do her own bit of scrutinising. And, like George, she found herself amazed… The man sitting at the impressive oak desk, in this expensively furnished office was George, but definitely not the teenager she remembered – this was the high-powered George she'd read about in the weekend colour supplements. This strikingly handsome man in his discreetly stylish Savile Row suit was master of himself and a celebrated media success story.

It was inevitable that George should offer her the job. She had the best qualifications of any applicant.

He'd resolutely not allowed himself to be influenced by her appearance, although he privately acknowledged that if she continued wearing that alluring Chanel No 5 perfume, he'd find it extremely distracting.

They were never quite sure when they fell in love. Sometimes, they wondered, if deep down, they'd been in love ever since school. One night, walking back to George's Porsche, dirty, tired and hungry after a long, hard day's shoot, George went directly from one sentence about lighting effects to an equally even-toned, "Marry me, Ella!"

"Yes, George." Her tone exactly matched his and it was a full thirty seconds before they realised what they'd done and collapsed laughing and crying into each other's arms.

"It was when he called me Ella," she was to say later, "after months of calling me Fenella, that I just knew it was right."

Just as it had been, back at Worthington Knight Comprehensive School, and later in the studio, they were a winning combination. A celeb wedding at St. George's, Hanover Square sealed their union and satisfied hordes of fans. The purchase of the old manor at Little Brassington provided them with the retreat they both craved and their happiness was made complete with the birth of a baby daughter, Prudence Guzell, in memory of a Gran who had always "been there" for George.

☺☺☺☺☺

"Pleased with the series?" Fenella looked up at him, smiling. It was an unnecessary question as they'd watched the last programme together earlier that day and given it the thumbs-up.

He nodded.

"Will you take a proper break now?" Her voice was slightly anxious and he recognised that this was where the conversation was really heading and hesitated.

"I thought I might get on with the book. Good opportunity and all that..."

"George Guzell! You're... you're incorrigible. A string of best-sellers to your name – a column in a Sunday broadsheet – never mind one TV series after another – a lecture tour of the States in the offing and..." she ran out of breath, "...and to hear you talk, it's as if you've never done anything... You're a glutton, you know," she paused again and this time they both howled with delight before she concluded – "for work."

But when the laughter subsided, George was thoughtfully quiet. A connoisseur, not only of good food, but also of wine, music and the arts, he had nothing to prove to himself or Fenella. Once they'd shared a desire to change the world. Now, they shared everything the world had to offer.

So, he knew Fenella was right, even if she'd only spoken in jest. Somewhere, deep inside, he was still that greedy little boy. Only this time, he wasn't killing himself. Instead, he'd channelled his huge appetite into creating a richly flavoured life of learning, work and family.

And as Great Grandfather Mortimer would have said, this time he did it "with R-E-S-P-E-C-T."

❋❋❋

Useful links

www.bbc.co.uk/health/conditions/obesity2.shtml

www.dailymail.co.uk/health/article-373437/Slimming-clubs-admit-11-year-olds.html

www.eco-schools.org.uk

www.foodafactoflife.org.uk/

www.foodforlife.org.uk

www.foodinschools.org/index.php

hcd2.bupa.co.uk/fact_sheets/html/child_obesity.html

www.healthyschools.gov.uk

www.jamieoliver.com/school-dinners

www.nhs.uk/Change4Life

www.nationalobesityforum.org.uk/content/blogcategory/23/176/

www.schoolfoodmatters.com/links

www.schoolfoodtrust.org.uk

www.teachernet.gov.uk/wholeschool/healthyliving/obesity/

www.thinkfoodandfarming.org.uk

If you enjoyed reading *Junk Food Hero* why not try

Letters from Alain
by Enriqué Perez Diaz

Arturo, a 12 year old boy lives on the island of Cuba. One day, his best friend Alain goes away with his family on a small boat, in search of a better life in America. But the sea can be a perilous place... When Alain's dog returns mysteriously, the adults fear the worst. But Arturo begins to receive strange letters from his friend. What do they mean? And will his friend ever return? The poignant tale of a child coming to terms with the realities of a troubled society.

ISBN
9780955156649
£6.99

Thistown
by Malcolm McKay

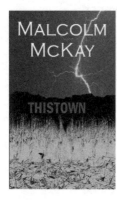

Somewhere beyond the rain, the wind and the stars, and as far from the Earth as it's possible to be, there was a town so old no one can remember how or when it began. It was a town where everyone remained exactly the same, a town where no one grew older, a town surrounded by a million miles of yellow corn, so strange that if you went in you disappeared immediately. And perhaps the town would have stayed the same if they hadn't found the Sleeping Man.

ISBN
0954691253
£7.99

He changed everything. Forever.